Books by L.M. Somerton

Elemental Hope

ISBN # 978-1-78686-303-4

©Copyright L.M. Somerton 2017

Cover Art by Posh Gosh ©Copyright 2017

Interior text design by Claire Siemaszkiewicz

Pride Publishing

Published in 2017 by Pride Publishing, Think Tank, Ruston Way, Lincoln, LN6 7FL, United Kingdom.

Pride Publishing is a subsidiary of Totally Entwined Group Limited.

Warlocks

ELEMENTAL HOPE

L.M. SOMERTON

Dedication

For anyone who yearns for a little magic in their life.

Chapter One

Nathaniel Alberich adjusted his position to get more comfortable on the rocky ground. There was a particularly sharp stone that seemed to have a magnetic attraction to his ass and no matter which way he shuffled, the damn thing followed right along. He allowed himself a self-indulgent moment to recall the comfortable leather chair in his office — well-cushioned and rock-free. The wild outdoors was not his preferred environment but on this occasion his location — on a mountaintop — was necessary. He narrowed his eyes, squinting at the stormy vista. Dark gray clouds edged with purple scudded past. Someone, somewhere, was going to be treated to a nice deluge. Nathaniel shrugged, winced then rolled some of the stiffness from his shoulders. It was about time he booked an appointment with his masseur. The man was a sadist, something Nathaniel could appreciate, but the pain he inflicted always resulted in looser limbs and unknotted muscles.

"All this stress is not good for me," Nathaniel muttered, aiming his complaint at a passing buzzard. The bird drifted lazily on currents of air Nathaniel fought hard to provide. He stood, flexing his fingers. He widened his stance and locked his knees in place. He didn't need the indignity of falling on his already bruised rear even if there was no one to witness his humiliation. He held his arms out then twisted his fingers into shapes that should have been impossible. Muttering incantations beneath his breath, he focused his will before expelling his power with a mental push. Around him the wind screamed in protest but the currents changed direction as he commanded. On the plains below, row after row of megalithic turbines started to rotate.

"Better. Much better." Nathaniel's thigh muscles trembled and pain stabbed behind his eyes. Using his power without a partner to channel through was uncomfortable. He'd learned to live with it over the years, channeling a fraction of the energy through anyone in the area. People nearby might experience a shiver, a mild headache or slight nausea. Nothing to attract undue attention. It wasn't enough, though, and without being able to dissipate the backlash of the forces he unleashed, Nathaniel suffered a great deal more than his unwitting assistants. He refused to give in to it. His business relied on his ability to work magic and along with it the jobs of thousands of employees. He couldn't let them down. He fought back the urge to vomit, pressing his knuckles into his temples until the spots in front of his eyes faded. The two-hour hike back to his car would help clear his head but he had no desire to break a limb on his way down the mountain.

After a few minutes of deep breathing he felt recovered enough to start walking. The trail was steep but he was well equipped with top-of-the-line boots. It wasn't his first trip to the peak and he'd learned from experience to come prepared for anything. He carried a small backpack containing bottled water and energy bars. A thick jacket and a pair of weatherproof pants — great against the elements, not so functional against pointy stones — ensured he stayed warm. The downward trip was still a slog and Nathaniel gave thanks for the many hours he'd spent in his home gym building stamina. Magic burned calories better than any sweaty spin class but he still needed to swim and run to keep up his fitness levels. It was a matter of survival, not vanity — and that was excellent motivation.

After a couple of hours, the path leveled out and Nathaniel covered the last half-mile quickly. On an unpaved road normally reserved for maintenance vehicles sat his gleaming Bentley Continental. There was no trace of the thick coating of dust it had collected earlier that day and his driver was leaning against the highly polished exterior. Nathaniel shook his head as he approached.

"Hey, Felix."

"Welcome back, sir."

"I've told you a thousand times to call me Nathaniel. You make me feel like my grandfather. I'm thirty-one, not a hundred and one."

"And your grandfather has long since passed, sir." Felix flicked a speck of dust from his pristine white cuff. "How are you feeling?"

"You mean for a warlock who's just manipulated the elements?"

"Precisely, sir."

"Like crap. I think that sums it up."

Felix frowned. "You know I'd help more if I could, sir."

"I know." Nathaniel sighed. "And if you ever fancy batting for my team for a change, you let me know. In the meantime, I'll manage."

Felix raised a blond eyebrow. He twitched his lips into a smile. "I'm not your type, even if I were…so inclined."

Nathaniel gave his fair, blue-eyed driver an appraising examination. He matched Nathaniel's height of six feet two and had broader shoulders as well as bigger muscles. There was no question he was handsome, and Nathaniel could appreciate him as a fine specimen of manhood, but he preferred his partners small, dark-eyed and submissive. Felix would never fit the bill.

"Sadly, that's true." He shrugged. "Now tell me how the fuck you managed to clean the car out here, and why you bothered when it's just going to get dirty again."

"Drivers never reveal their secrets, sir."

"Or those of their employers." It wasn't a question. Nathaniel trusted Felix implicitly. He'd been with him since Nathaniel had come into his power at twenty-one. He was a friend, a confidant and utterly indispensable. Felix gave his usual enigmatic smile and opened the car door.

"Why don't you get in before you collapse and I have to

haul your heavy ass in there? Sir."

Nathaniel rolled his eyes at Felix's insubordination but scrambled into the passenger seat anyway. It was good to get the weight off his legs. He reclined the back a little then relaxed into the leather with a relieved sigh. Felix got behind the wheel, closing his door gently. The two of them were cocooned in temperature-controlled luxury.

"You should sit in the back," Felix said, turning the key in the ignition.

"And you say that every time I get in the damn car. I never sit in the back." Nathaniel closed his eyes. "Take me home, Felix. It's been one long-assed day."

It was a three hundred and some mile trip from Tehachapi back to Atherton, where Nathaniel had his main residence. Felix usually managed it in a miraculous four hours or so but Nathaniel was glad they only needed to make the trip once a month. His other wind farms were closer to home. Every time he tweaked the elements in his favor, the power he expended left him drained. Without Felix to shepherd him back to the house, he would have to camp out until he regained his strength.

"God forbid," Nathaniel muttered under his breath.

"Dreaming of tents and the great outdoors again?" Felix's tone no doubt reflected the smirk on his face, but Nathaniel couldn't be bothered to open his eyes and check.

"I need to get less predictable."

"You need to rest."

Nathaniel grunted. There was no way he was going to give Felix credit for being right. The steady thrum of the Bentley's engine soon lulled him into a doze but it was hard to rest. Channeling his power through so many anonymous bodies always left him unsettled and twitchy. It allowed him to work without the need to vent every other day, but was nowhere near as effective as if he had a life partner to take some of the strain. His semi-waking dreams let him picture who that man might be. Someone eager to please but with an energetic spark. Independent, but willing to be taken care of. Submissive in the bedroom and able to deal with the unique needs of a sometimes-cranky control-freak of a warlock. And there was the problem. The whole warlock thing was a major road block to finding the right man. Any man.

A sudden, sharp pain speared Nathaniel's temple. "Fuck!" He jerked into full consciousness. "What the hell?" He knuckled his head in an attempt to ease the pain.

"What's up?" Felix asked, sounding concerned. "You're white as a sheet. Do you need me to stop somewhere?"

Nathaniel took a couple of cleansing deep breaths and the pain receded. "No, it's okay. Someone's messing with the elements. Someone with vast power. I've felt this a few times in recent months." His stomach churned. "Perhaps we *should* stop. I need some air. And it's about time I gave Gregory Thanet a call. Apparently we have things to discuss."

Felix pulled off the road at the next rest stop, bought a couple of coffees at the drive-thru then parked next to a grassy area where a few wooden picnic tables were set out. Nathaniel got out of the car and had to lean on the door for a few seconds.

"You need a hand?" Felix called.

"No. I'm just a bit dizzy. It's passing." Nathaniel took a few deep breaths. "I'll sit at one of the tables and make my call."

"Sure thing." Felix reclined his seat a few inches. "Knock yourself out. Well, don't…because then I'd have to come rescue your ass, but you know what I mean."

Nathaniel slammed the door on him. He hauled himself to the nearest table then sat, straddling the bench seat for stability. After extracting his phone from his pocket, he scrolled through the contacts. He hadn't spoken to Gregory Thanet in a while but they did keep in touch, albeit infrequently. On the occasions they talked it was often to share their mutual disgust for the behavior of the third warlock on the continent, Symeon Malus. Nathaniel dialed Gregory's number. He waited for the call to connect, sipping his coffee.

"This is Gregory."

"Good to know you're still not into effusive greetings, old friend." Nathaniel rolled his shoulders to ease some tension. One of his joints popped.

"Nathaniel. It's been a while. I can surmise the reason for your call. I assume you've been experiencing some... fluctuations in the elements?"

"How could I not? What the hell is going on, Gregory? I just had a metal spike driven through my brain, and now I feel hungover without the benefit of getting wasted first."

"It was quite a jolt, wasn't it?"

"Quite a... That's like saying Hurricane Katrina was a mild breeze."

"Yes, I suppose that's true."

"Gregory, is there someone new on the scene or is Symeon up to something? I didn't think that snake had it in him."

"He doesn't...anymore." Gregory sighed. "Three have become four, Nathaniel, and I have a lot to bring you up to speed on."

"What do you mean, anymore? And who, how?" Nathaniel asked, feeling like he'd departed to an alternate reality.

"My godson, Evrain. What you felt just now was him venting. He's also had to deal with Symeon's latest misdeeds, with a bit of assistance from me. He hasn't learned to buffer the rest of us from the effects of his power yet. He's still quite wild."

"Holy fuck. I thought Evrain was just a kid? You shielded him, didn't you?"

"Agatha did and he fought it all the way. Look, Nathaniel, I know you're busy, but do you think you could fit in a visit? I have far too much to tell you during a phone call and I should apologize for not getting in touch sooner. Evrain is living at Hornbeam Cottage, Agatha's old place, but I'd happily put you up in Portland. Coryn and I are spending a lot of time there at the moment."

Nathaniel grunted. "I'm sure your boy *needs* a lot of support."

"He does. He's a quick study, but he has a long way to go. He's not exactly…pliable when it comes to his training."

"Well, as it happens, I am free for a few days. I suppose I could dig out some rain gear."

"It doesn't rain *all* the time in Oregon."

Nathaniel didn't credit that with a response. "Can you book a room for Felix as well? He won't want to miss out on all the fun."

"How is that man still putting up with you?"

"I put a spell on him."

"Felix is immune."

"More's the pity." Nathaniel chuckled. "He'd be a lot less opinionated if I could work a little magic on him. He's waiting for me now, so I'd better go. Text me the hotel details when you have them. We'll see you in two days. I'll give you a call when we arrive."

"Sure. Coryn and I will look forward to it."

Nathaniel disconnected the call. He stared at the few puffs of cotton wool dancing across the sky. "I know where you're heading," he muttered. "Portland."

Chapter Two

Dominic Castine sat at the small garden table in a sheltered spot and tilted his face toward the sun. It was still early but promised to be a warm day for once. The heat on his skin was welcome and he pushed the fall of his hair back to expose more skin. He unfastened the two top buttons of his loose cotton shirt, which he wore over faded jeans. It was tempting to go shirtless but his pale skin was prone to burning and he hadn't applied any sunscreen yet. He curled his bare toes into the cool grass, smiling at the slight tickle. A sense of peace enveloped him, the only sounds the rustle of leaves and the twittering of birds. He knew the instant Evrain rounded the corner of the cottage. The whole world betrayed him. Tree branches swayed in arboreal excitement and the birds went into paroxysms of ecstasy. A swirling breeze lifted Dominic's shirt, exposing his belly. He rolled his eyes then raised them to meet his lover's green gaze.

"Showoff." Dominic reached for the pot of fresh coffee Evrain carried. He put it safely on the table before Evrain's powers set the liquid inside to boiling. "I hope this is decaffeinated because you really don't need the boost this morning."

Evrain raised one dark eyebrow. Dominic withstood his scrutiny, though it took some courage to maintain eye contact.

"If things around here are a little...worked up, that is entirely down to you," Evrain said.

Dominic couldn't decide if it was threat or promise in Evrain's tone but his cock responded as it always did, plumping into life. "How can you possibly blame me for your witchy-boy ways?" He wiggled his fingers in a vague imitation of Evrain's movements when he was spellcasting.

"Because you sit there, shining like the sun, and you never fail to take my breath away."

Dominic's breath hitched.

"You're also a cheeky brat in need of a good spanking." Evrain grabbed a fistful of Dominic's hair then tugged his head back. He leaned close, the scent of his breath a familiar mixture of peppermint and coffee. "You're too gorgeous to resist."

Dominic parted his lips, expecting a kiss, but Evrain pulled away. He wagged his finger.

"Oh no, you have to earn it." He took a seat then poured himself a mug of coffee. A plate of sliced fruit sat in the middle of the table. He took a sliver of apple. Dominic watched, entranced, as Evrain bit into the fruit. The juice wetted his lips, making them gleam.

"What do you want me to do?" Even as he asked the question, a thrill of expectation rippled the length of Dominic's spine.

"Stand up." Evrain pointed to a spot on the grass in front of him.

Dominic sank his teeth into his bottom lip but complied. He stood in position, hands loosely clasped behind his back.

"Take your shirt off." Evrain's eyes glinted green and gold. "Slowly."

Fingers trembling, Dominic unfastened the rest of his buttons. He shrugged the fabric from his shoulders and let it fall to the ground.

"Hands behind your back again." Evrain bent forward and plucked a couple of daisies. He got to his feet. "It's hard to improve on perfection, but I think I have a way." He flicked one of Dominic's exposed nipples. The sharp sting made Dominic gasp. He took an involuntary step back.

"Keep still. Your body is mine, to do with as I please, and it pleases me to make you squirm."

Dominic locked his knees. He should object to Evrain's

arrogant claim but he only spoke the truth. He stood still and tried not to flinch as Evrain subjected his nipples to more abuse. They stood hard and proud, the delicious ache connected directly to his cock. Evrain laid one of the flowers he'd picked against Dominic's chest. He closed his eyes and muttered a few words under his breath, and his fingers twitched. The daisy's slender stem wound around Dominic's nub in a tight spiral, squeezing the already tender flesh. The flower rested in place, firmly secured. Then Evrain repeated the process with the other nipple. The bindings were just as effective as any clamp. Dominic took shallow breaths, dealing with the erotic pain as best he could.

Evrain smirked as he resumed his seat.

"You are far too pleased with yourself." Dominic resisted the urge to tear at the constricting stems.

"Quiet, sweetheart. There are plenty of things out here I could gag you with. Now — trousers off."

"When are you going to start calling them pants?" Dominic unfastened the stud at his waistband then lowered his zipper.

"Pants are underwear, something I suspect you aren't wearing." Evrain's grin was feral.

He was right. Again. Dominic sighed but pushed his jeans down to his ankles then kicked them off his bare feet. The movement jolted his chest, giving him a painful reminder of his bound nipples. His cock jerked. Evrain licked his lips.

"I would never condone what Symeon did to you, love, but I have to admit to liking the fur-free look."

Dominic's cheeks heated. His hairless groin was a permanent reminder of his treatment at Symeon Malus' hands. Apart from the burnished copper waves on his head, eyebrows and eyelashes, the rest of his body was entirely hair free. Not having to shave was poor compensation.

"Of course, I would prefer to shave you myself. That would be fun." Evrain drummed his fingers on one thigh. "Would you be still for me, sweetheart, if I had a blade that close to your balls?"

Dominic shivered. The thought of Evrain baring him that way was highly erotic. As was standing naked in the open air in front of his fully clothed boyfriend. "Isn't Gregory coming this morning? I don't really want him to find me like this, Evrain."

"We have plenty of time for what I have in mind." Evrain lowered his fly, letting his cock poke through the opening. "Come here."

Dominic took a few paces forward to straddle Evrain's thighs. Evrain took a firm hold of Dominic's dick and gave it a few tugs. "Keep your hands behind your back." He reached down the side of his chair to pluck a long piece of grass. A few whispered words and Dominic discovered that a single blade could become an effective cock ring when magically bound around the base of his balls. Plant sap also provided a ready source of lubricant, something that Dominic was grateful for as Evrain tugged him forward.

"This stuff tingles," Evrain said, slathering his shaft in viscous liquid.

"I appreciate your sacrifice."

"Sarcasm is unbecoming in one so young. I want you impaled on my cock. Now."

Evrain dug his fingers into Dominic's ass, compelling him downward. Dominic didn't resist. Without preparation, penetration burned a little but it had only been a few hours since they'd last made love and he was still quite slick. He grunted as his ass met Evrain's thighs. He felt so full and the pressure on his prostate was unbearable. He had to move. He attempted to rise but Evrain held him in place for a few torturous seconds. He pulled his head down for a bruising kiss, which left Dominic gasping.

"Now, you can fuck yourself on me."

Without the use of his hands for balance, the rise and fall motion Dominic managed was uncoordinated and jerky. Evrain let him struggle, staring into his eyes, then took control.

"Hold on to my shoulders."

Dominic obeyed eagerly. He was desperate to come and only the makeshift cock ring was preventing his orgasm. The frustration was torment.

"Please, Evrain…"

Evrain grunted and thrust hard into his channel.

"Please!" As the wet heat of Evrain's release filled Dominic's passage, Evrain snapped the grass ring around Dominic's balls with a word, allowing him to come. At last. His orgasm surged through him, his cum splattering Evrain's shirt. His vision blurred and only Evrain's hold kept him from losing his balance. He panted hard, sweat cooling on his skin. Evrain brushed a few strands of hair away from his face.

"Take a breath, sweetheart."

The stems around his nipples fell away. The flood of sudden pain made him scream and come again, his body jerking. Exhausted, he slumped against Evrain. "You son of a bitch," he muttered.

"You still love me." Evrain sucked on his neck.

"You're marking me." Dominic didn't object.

"Because you're mine. You need a collar of love bites."

"You don't have time for that. I should dress. Gregory will be here any minute."

Evrain groaned. "Don't remind me. What possessed me to agree to his training regime? The man's a sadist."

"Takes one to know one." Dominic stood, legs shaking. He grabbed his clothes. "Here, wear my shirt. I'll take yours inside. I'm going to take another shower." He threw his shirt to Evrain, who stripped off his own soiled garment. Dominic allowed himself a moment to admire the smooth planes of Evrain's body. Considering he never ventured near a gym, Dominic was convinced his lover used spellcraft to stay in shape.

Reluctantly, he went inside to shower and change. His ass twinged, making him smile. Evrain sure knew how to start the day with a bang. Wearing fresh jeans and a soft T-shirt,

Dominic wandered back outside to collect the remains of their breakfast. Evrain was lounging in his seat, nibbling pieces of fruit.

"You gave me an appetite, love." He stood and Dominic walked into his arms.

Anyone with the ability to see would have witnessed the aura of power around Evrain sparking furiously. Dominic knew it was happening. It didn't take magical ability to notice the sudden gusts in the wind or the lashing of the branches in nearby trees. He was subjected to a kiss that was all about domination. He put up no resistance. Evrain was a force of nature and not to be denied. Dominic leaned into Evrain's strong hold.

"I love you, Evrain."

"I love you too." Evrain's deep voice vibrated with passion. "I don't deserve you."

"Don't be an idiot."

Evrain kissed him again, long and slow, slipping one hand down to cup his ass. "Mmm. More punishment for you later."

"If you have the energy once Gregory is done with you." Dominic rested his head on Evrain's shoulder and smiled at the silver-haired man approaching the gate.

"Evrain! Put that poor boy down and get your incompetent butt over here! We have work to do."

Dominic shook with laughter.

"Shit." Evrain turned into his godfather's intimidating glare. Gregory was standing by the garden gate, tapping his long fingers impatiently against the rough wood. His expression softened when he met Dominic's eyes. Dominic imagined his tousled, damp hair and kiss-bruised lips told their own story.

"Good morning, Dominic."

"Hello, Gregory. You're early." Dominic grinned. He liked Evrain's godfather and his partner Coryn a lot. They were always kind to him and treated him like an equal despite Gregory being another powerful warlock. As Gregory's life partner, Coryn was one of the few men alive who could understand Dominic's position and what he went through every time Evrain used him to channel his power. Evrain, however, they handled with less sensitivity. Gregory had extracted Evrain's promise that he would accept training from him and he took that promise very seriously. He imposed the harshest discipline and Evrain was expected to accept his word as law. Love was at the root of it, Dominic knew. Training Evrain to use his prodigious talent could be the difference between life and death for both of them. Dominic could tell Evrain hated it, but he submitted anyway, keeping his dominant nature at bay.

"It is fortunate that I wasn't here any sooner, I can see." Gregory scowled in Evrain's direction. "What are you waiting for, boy? We have a long day ahead of us. I hope you haven't exerted too much energy already."

Evrain squared his shoulders with a sigh, straightened his clothing then walked toward his godfather. Dominic gave a low chuckle and received a scowl in return along with a muttered, "I'll deal with you later."

Dominic turned to the garden. He strolled to the shed that housed most of his hand tools. He unlatched the door and let it swing open. The scent of earth and wood enveloped him. He breathed deeply, the familiarity of it comforting. A small spider dropped from its web on a line of almost invisible silk to dangle in front of his face.

"Well, hi there." Dominic ducked under the spider. His favorite spade was propped against the wall. He rubbed his hand along the smooth grain of the wooden handle—it was warm to the touch. He'd always found he preferred tools made from more traditional materials. They were heavier but felt better in his hands. He picked up the spade then left the cool dark of the shed and returned to the sunshine. At the back of the property was a large plot he planned to dig over ready for late summer planting. Monotonous, heavy work would help him when Evrain began to channel, which he was doing more and more in his sessions with Gregory.

He picked a spot to start, stamped the spade into the earth and waited for the pain to begin. It didn't remove his ability to work but the sensation was nowhere near as enjoyable as the erotic pain Evrain inflicted. For that, Dominic had a much higher threshold. His nipples twinged at the thought, making him smile.

Evrain followed Gregory to the other side of the cottage where a small copse of trees stood alongside a field of rough grass. A stream bubbled at its far end, water bouncing across stones polished to a diamond shine. In the center of the field two huge, granite boulders sat brooding — the lone remnants of an ancient medicine wheel, as Gregory called it. 'Stone circle' was the term Evrain recognized.

"Your grandmother and many generations of your family have lived here for good reason, Evrain," Gregory said. "The confluence of ley lines beneath the stones provides a valuable source of restorative power."

"I know. My grandmother spoke of it repeatedly. She used to come and sit out here a lot." Evrain trailed his fingers across one of the stones. "You haven't brought me out here before."

"Things are changing, Evrain. It's a good place to train you. It should help your focus considerably and we need to move things along." His forehead creased into a frown. "Now, I want to see your warm-up exercises. I do hope you've been practicing." Gregory sat on the ground with his back against a boulder. He crossed his ankles, looking for all the world like he was on a relaxing day out. All he needed was a Thermos flask and picnic basket to complete the picture.

Evrain rolled his eyes but held back the sarcastic retort that rose too freely to his lips. He calmed his thoughts then started to manipulate his fingers, twisting them into shape after shape. Glistening droplets of water formed in the air. They hovered in place while tiny flames appeared alongside them. Wisps of wind formed miniature tornadoes, dancing and spinning. Evrain braced himself, legs set apart. He changed his movements a fraction and a dozen small stones rose from the ground to join the display. It took intense concentration to manipulate all four elements at the same time. Beads of perspiration broke out on his forehead as his fingers flickered faster and faster. He couldn't stop to wipe the moisture away. Unless he channeled, this was the physical equivalent of running a marathon with a bag full of rocks strapped to his back.

Gregory gave a heavy sigh and got to his feet. He walked around Evrain in a slow circle, then his long fingers flickered into action and tiny sparks began to hit Evrain's exposed skin, his face, neck and hands. Yelping, he lost concentration and stumbled. The flames extinguished, pebbles dropped to the ground and an uncontrolled gust of wind blew the water droplets into his face.

"Fuck it!" He batted at his skin where the sparks had hit him, rubbing away the small hurts. Impatiently, he wiped water and sweat from his face and glowered at Gregory.

"Adjust your attitude, boy. Look at me with respect."

Evrain kicked at the ground. He didn't appreciate being called a boy but knew that to Gregory he was just that. He cast his eyes down. "I apologize."

Gregory grunted his acceptance of the apology. "You are too easily distracted. You lack discipline. If you cannot master even these simple tasks, how do you expect to control your full strength? You have too much power to be careless, Evrain." He squeezed Evrain's shoulder lightly. "Why didn't you channel?"

"Because I don't want to hurt Dominic unless I really have to."

"I'm afraid you do have to. Just as I hurt Coryn—though he barely feels me after all these years."

"The sensation fades?" Evrain was genuinely curious.

"It did for Coryn and I'm sure it will for Dominic. Does he suffer greatly?"

"He says not." Evrain scuffed his foot into the grass. "I

don't believe him."

"Well, you should. Dominic's not the kind to lie just to salve your delicate feelings. He understands his role and has accepted it. He knows you love him."

"I feel like I'm using him."

"You are. I'm not going to pretty it up for you, Evrain. But you need him and he has the strength to be there for you. You have to trust him just as he trusts you."

Evrain knew it was true. He nodded.

"Good. Now take your shirt off. I'm an old man and I need a bigger target."

"Charming." Evrain stripped off Dominic's shirt, immediately mourning the loss of his scent. Ferns rose around his ankles. They twisted around his calves, holding him in place.

"To help you balance." Gregory gestured at the fronds, which tightened further. "Begin your exercises again."

This time there was no delay before Gregory began to fire sparks at Evrain's body. Everywhere they touched, his pale skin was marked with a small red welt. Soon his shoulders, back and chest were dotted with the marks. He kept his expression cold, ignored the pain and juggled the elements skillfully. He channeled his power and his performance showed a marked improvement. It was still ten minutes before Gregory relented.

"Okay, that's enough. Better. Not perfect but better. I want you to practice every day."

Evrain let out his breath with a shudder. The salt of his sweat was making every weal sting. Fatigue permeated each cell of his body.

"You need to be able to do that as easily as you breathe, Evrain." Gregory had his hands on his hips, his expression stern. "I've told you before how fit you need to be to wield the power. Do you ever listen to me?"

Evrain stood in silence as Gregory continued to berate him. He had the sense to realize it was worth putting up with the abuse. Gregory was an excellent teacher and his help was worth every scolding. The ferns around Evrain's ankles unwound but he stayed where he was. He met Gregory's eyes and flinched. "I do listen, I promise. I'll do better."

"I don't enjoy being so hard on you, Evrain, but it *is* necessary."

"I know." Evrain had a strange urge to comfort his godfather. "I understand, even if I'm not very good at showing it. We're men. We're not supposed to get this touchy feely."

"So true." Gregory moved to position himself behind one of the standing stones. "So let's get on, shall we? I want you to draw water from the ground then draw it through the granite." He touched the top of the stone, which stood around four feet high. "I want to see a pool of liquid in this indentation."

Evrain stared at him in disbelief. It was the most difficult thing Gregory had ever asked him to do. Evrain could turn a burbling stream into a raging torrent, change a smoldering fire into an inferno, bend the earth to his will, but all those things took raw power rather than control. This meant manipulating earth and water together at a molecular level. It would need all his strength and discipline. He didn't really believe he could do it, but he had to try.

Evrain closed his eyes and channeled, searching for the strength that came from his emotional connection to Dominic. It was hard to explain how it affected him. He could sense the beat of Dominic's heart and every pulse sent a charge of energy through him. His senses all seemed sharper, his mind clearer. He could feel the power within him and the connection strengthened his ability to exert his will over something wild and unpredictable. He let his senses explore, moving earth and rock aside to allow a tiny tributary of the stream at the end of the field to form. He created the narrowest of passages for it, sending it underground. He nudged aside earthworms and redirected a confused velvet-black mole. The water seeped its way in increments across the field. Time stood still as Evrain moved each root and burrowing insect. He imposed his will on earth, air and water. After a while, he dropped to his knees and concentrated on the particles of the rock in front of him, separating each tiny crystal in his mind, creating a channel for liquid to pass through. He coaxed the liquid bead by bead until finally, moisture appeared on the top of the huge boulder, formed a small pool then trickled silver back to the earth as it overflowed.

Exhausted, Evrain fell forward onto his hands. He focused on the blades of soft grass beneath his palms and looked on, bewildered as a dark red droplet splashed against the green. He raised trembling fingers to his nose. They came away stained red. He shivered. Whilst completing his task he hadn't noticed the temperature at all, but now the air felt cool against his bare skin.

A pile of white cloth landed in front of him. It took him a few moments to work out that it was his discarded shirt. He pulled it on, fumbling with the buttons. Slowly he took in the dimming light and registered that the whole day had gone by. Gregory lounged, cross-legged, in the grass, chewing on a single juicy stalk.

"Maybe you have learned a thing or two." He climbed to his feet and turned toward the lane. "You're pale as a ghost. Get inside and eat. I'll see you again tomorrow and I'll be bringing a guest."

"Who?" Evrain wasn't feeling in the least bit sociable. He wiped the back of his hand across his face, smearing it with blood.

"Nathaniel Alberich. I spoke to him yesterday and he's very keen to meet you."

"The fourth warlock?" Evrain's curiosity sparked.

"Yes. He's been sensing your power. He's nothing like Symeon. I consider him a friend and ally. I think you'll like him." A trace of a smile crossed his lips. "Go home and give Dominic a hug. He's going to need it." Gregory got to his feet. "Wait, I have something for you." He dug in his pocket, pulling out a length of cord with a star-shaped pendant attached. "Give this to Dominic to wear. He should never take it off. It will provide some protection for him outside the cottage wards. It's identical to one that Coryn has. It won't stop physical harm but it will guard against spellcraft."

Evrain wound the cord around his fingers, wishing the pendant was attached to a chain he could padlock around Dominic's neck. "I'll make sure he wears it."

"Don't frighten him too much, Evrain. We have many enemies but he doesn't need to live in fear. It's your job to look out for him as best you can." Gregory strolled away with a brief wave and a smile.

Evrain watched him go, wishing he had the energy to ask more questions about the pendant, about Nathaniel Alberich or just to utter a few choice curses.

"Dominic." Evrain was still on his knees so he hauled himself to his feet. He had been channeling for something like eight hours and he felt like death, but he had been in control of his own actions. He had used Dominic mercilessly and felt sick at the thought. He managed a stumbling run to the cottage, where a cozy glow promised warmth and refuge.

Evrain shoved open the door. Dominic was sitting in one of the armchairs next to the fire, which had burned down to glowing embers. He was reading one of Agatha's old books on herbal lore, the green cover faded with age. He looked up with a gentle smile, blue eyes sparkling in the glow of dying fire.

"You look terrible. Come and sit down and I'll make you a drink and something to eat."

Evrain leaned against the doorframe, resting his head against the wood. "You're all right?" He was afraid to get any closer in case proximity allowed him to identify signs of pain on Dominic's beautiful face.

"Shut the door, you're letting in the cold." Dominic laid his book to one side after marking his place with a stem of dried herbs. "Come and sit down before you fall over."

Evrain was being cajoled like a child who knew he'd done something wrong and didn't want to face the consequences.

"I'm fine. Really." Dominic beckoned him over.

Evrain walked toward him, noting his pallor. "Don't lie to me, Dominic. I need to know how you really feel." He put every ounce of command he could manage into his words. Dominic sighed.

"Fine. As you'll drive me nuts pestering me to tell you." He shifted in his seat. "It's a kind of bone-deep ache that permeates every part of my body. Something like when you have the flu. I worked on the garden until it became too much to ignore then moved inside. Herbal tea and the warmth of the fire have helped, because for some reason I was cold despite the sunshine. As long as I don't try to move around too much, it's manageable."

Evrain ran a hand through his hair. "I hate hurting you."

"You know, it's strange. I knew the instant you stopped channeling and I missed the intimacy of the connection. Then there's relief as the ache reduces. I'm pretty sure that what I'm feeling now is the result of muscles strained by tension. I'm going to have to teach myself some relaxation techniques. Do you think Coryn would be able to help me with that?"

"I'm sure he would. Gregory says he barely feels anything after all the years they've been together. He thinks it will get better over time for you too."

Evrain sat in the other chair, enjoying the residual warmth of the fire. Dominic bent forward and placed a hand gently on his knee.

"Gregory was hard on you today."

Evrain met Dominic's questioning eyes. He nodded. "Unfortunately, he needs to be. I don't have to like it. I do have to put up with it."

Dominic got up and planted a soft kiss on Evrain's lips, "Yes, you do. Anything that keeps you safe is fine with me."

Evrain reached up and grabbed his hair, pulling him

down for a much harder kiss, crushing Dominic's lips with his own, raking his smooth cheek with rough stubble. "You're not completely exhausted then?" Dominic asked the question while backing toward the kitchen with a lazy, wicked smile. Evrain raised his eyebrows. That slightly insolent expression was more usual on his face than Dominic's. It was a challenge — one Evrain's cock was more than happy to rise to.

"You think you're in control now, do you?" Evrain stood to follow his lover.

"I wouldn't dare contemplate such a thing." Dominic's grin said otherwise.

"I was planning to pamper you this evening. Treat you to a bit of TLC after the day you've had." Evrain stalked him, gaze fixed on Dominic's obvious erection. "But I can see I need to take care of you another way."

Evrain let Dominic reverse until the back of his thighs hit the heavy oak of the kitchen table, then he pounced. He had him bent over the edge of the table, face pressed against the wood, his pants and underwear pooled around his ankles before he could draw breath to protest. Evrain didn't think his grandmother, Agatha, would have been amused at the alternative use of her table but there was no stopping what was about to happen.

He growled and kicked off his clothing until he was naked from the waist down. His dick was throbbing and hot, inspired by an inescapable need to claim what was his. To Evrain's smug satisfaction, Dominic didn't resist as his arms were pulled back behind him. Evrain circled his wrists with one hand and held them together with a firm grip. He used his bare foot to push Dominic's spread legs even wider apart. Dominic moaned when Evrain teased his hole with the head of his shaft. As far as Dominic knew, Evrain had no lubrication. Spontaneity didn't necessarily mean adequate preparation. Evrain loved that Dominic's trust that he wouldn't be hurt was so assured but he wouldn't dream of taking him dry. He slathered his cock in something that would do the job then jerked his hips forward, sliding smoothly into Dominic's receptive channel. Without stretching, Evrain knew that Dominic would feel the burn of such quick penetration. He also knew he liked it. His gasp wasn't one of pain. Evrain couldn't hold back. This was about driving need, about possession. It was wild and exciting.

"I love you." Evrain pistoned his hips back and forth, pushing Dominic against the table with every stroke. "So very much." It was difficult to speak but Evrain needed Dominic to know how deep his feelings ran. "When I'm inside you, when we're joined, there is nothing else. There will *be* no one else for me. Ever."

"Feels so good," Dominic gasped. "Love you too!"

"I'm the only man who will ever take you like this." Evrain paused. "Say it!"

"For pity's sake, Evrain! I only want you. Only you."

"Always?"

"Always."

The heat of victory filled Evrain. The whimpers and moans coming from beneath him spurred him on and he moved faster, gripping Dominic's waist with one hand, squeezing his wrists together with the other. Dominic, his cock rubbing against the table, came first with a scream and Evrain's name on his lips. Evrain followed as a last, violent thrust scattered stars in front of his eyes and forced a triumphant scream of release from his mouth.

He took a few gasping breaths and let his weight rest for a moment on Dominic's back. He had to force his finger cuff to relax, releasing Dominic's arms. Beneath him, Dominic trembled. Evrain stroked his flank.

"Stay put, sweetheart." Evrain withdrew carefully.

"Can't move anyway," Dominic mumbled. He raised his head briefly then laid it back on his arms. He took a few deep breaths and closed his eyes. Evrain crossed to the sink. He ran the hot water for a while, waiting until it warmed, then soaked a cloth. Returning to Dominic, he took a moment to admire the shiny trails leaking from his lover's ass.

"I'd like to leave this on your skin." He ran a finger across the back of Dominic's thigh.

"Too sticky."

"True." Evrain cleaned semen from Dominic's skin. "Okay, gorgeous, you can stand up now, though this view is delectable."

Dominic yanked up his underwear and pants. He sat on the edge of the table, swinging his legs. His face was flushed, his blue eyes even brighter than usual. He pushed his hair back from his face and met Evrain's anxious gaze.

"Did I hurt you?" Evrain asked. "I hardly knew what I was doing...but Christ, that was hot!"

"I think I might need a cushion for a while." Dominic blinked. "But you can do that any time you like."

"Oh, I will..." Evrain cupped a possessive hand around his neck and nipped at his lip before pushing his tongue forward to explore. He could feel Dominic shaking and pulled away. "You haven't eaten, have you?"

"I was waiting for you." Dominic's creamy skin was very pale.

"Idiot. Channeling is hard work for you as well as me. You must look after yourself." Evrain manhandled him into a chair then tousled his copper locks. "I'll make sandwiches." He paused, grinning. "Think I'd better get some new butter out, though." Dominic twisted his head to see and laughed at the deep gouge marks in the softening pat. Evrain shrugged. "It was the closest thing to hand."

Chapter Three

Dominic had a gardening job to go to the following morning. His internal alarm clock woke him, though the dawn chorus was so loud he wondered how Evrain could possibly stay asleep. He gave him a fond glance while he dressed, pulling on black cargoes and a dark green polo shirt, which formed a uniform of sorts. Dominic was still exhausted, the fatigue that came from channeling for Evrain deep within his bones. He could only imagine how much worse it must be for his lover. Evrain seemed younger, more innocent in sleep but tiny frown lines marred his forehead as if his dreams disturbed him.

Crawling back into bed seemed like a very good idea, but Dominic didn't want to let his customers down. He had to make a conscious effort to move, descending the stairs to the kitchen as quietly as possible. Mindful of Evrain's advice to look after himself better, he went to the trouble of putting together a filling breakfast of oatmeal and sliced banana, the drizzle of honey on the top an illicit indulgence. After that, and a couple of slices of whole-wheat toast thickly spread with butter, he felt much better. A steaming mug of peppermint tea washed it all down and he was ready to go.

He sensed rather than heard Evrain's approach, so didn't jump when Evrain hugged him from behind. He hummed his pleasure as Evrain nuzzled his neck.

"Hey, you. I tried to be quiet so you could carry on sleeping," Dominic said.

"You think I can sleep when you're not there next to me?" Evrain sniffed the air. "Is there coffee?"

"Sorry, no." Dominic lifted his mug. "I had tea."

"That is not tea," Evrain complained. "Tea is brown. You put milk in it. Not creamer. Milk. God, I miss decent tea. But now I need coffee." He ambled toward the shiny chrome machine on the worktop. His shorts hugged his ass in a very appealing manner. Dominic only got a glimpse because Evrain had a baggy T-shirt on over the top.

"Well, I have to leave you to your love affair with caffeine. I have customers waiting. Lawns to mow." He pushed his chair back.

"I have to work too, especially as we have visitors later today. You will be back, won't you?"

"Of course," Dominic said. "Where would I rather be than in a room full of warlocks?"

"Sarcasm equals spankings. Once I've had coffee."

Dominic edged toward the door. There was no way he was letting Evrain near him or he'd never leave.

"Wait!" Evrain grinned. "Don't worry, your ass is safe. For now. I have something for you. I meant to give it to you yesterday, but you distracted me." He ran up the stairs.

Dominic waited by the door, listening to random thumps from above. Evrain thudded back down the stairs. He had something dangling from his fingers. He crossed the room then held out his hand so that Dominic could see what was in it. It was a pendant of sorts, a small black star hanging from a narrow cord. Dominic took it. He'd thought the star was fashioned from metal because it was shiny, but it was actually made from polished stone. It was tactile and strangely warm.

"What kind of material is this?" he asked.

"It's called schorl."

"I've never heard of it."

"It's more commonly known as black tourmaline. Gregory gave it to me. Coryn has one too."

"Why? What's it for?"

"Protection."

Evrain took the pendant back then fastened the cord around Dominic's neck. The star lay in the hollow at the base of his throat.

"I want you to wear this at all times. It will protect you outside the gates. Promise me that you won't go out without it on."

Dominic looked at him, saw the resolve in his eyes and nodded. "I promise."

"You're not going to argue with me?" Evrain blinked.

"No. I can recognize a stubborn, immoveable object when I see one." Dominic touched the star. "It's warm. It will make me think of you when I'm working."

"You should be thinking of me anyway!" Evrain protested.

Dominic decided to make his escape while he still could, before Evrain got a caffeine boost and shrugged off the sleepiness that softened some of his hard edges. His work boots were just inside the door so he pulled them on, keeping one eye on Evrain, who was inhaling the aroma of fresh coffee beans.

"I'll see you later." Dominic had one hand on the door handle.

"Yes, you will." The gold flecks in Evrain's eyes glowed.

Dominic swallowed. There was a threat of punishment in that eerie gaze and his body responded to the idea of it with an enthusiasm he couldn't control.

The clock had yet to strike eight when he slipped outside, pulling the cottage door closed behind him. It was a cool morning but with the promise of warmth in the air. Dominic felt relaxed as he headed off down the lane to the pull-in where he parked his van. He knew that Evrain had a storyboard to finish this morning and was unlikely to be channeling until later when he would have to practice some of the exercises that Gregory always gave him. Hopefully that would give Dominic a pain-free day to deal with some of his regular clients.

Both his morning calls were local. His first call was to a widow who could no longer manage her extensive lawns. It was fortunate for him that she owned a ride-on mower. The job was routine but enhanced by homemade cookies and lemonade. He was at his second customer's house by ten and spent the next couple of hours weeding, trimming shrubs and tidying up a garden belonging to an elderly couple who sat and watched him work. They chatted away about their family and told him all the local gossip. Most of the time he had no clue who they were talking about but he was glad of their company. By the time he'd finished and cleaned up at the outside tap his stomach was beginning to rumble. He said his goodbyes then drove to the single local store, where the owner made him up a sandwich. The hamlet he was working in was close to a small lake so he drove to the parking area then took his sandwich and sat on a wooden bench to enjoy the sunshine. A couple of birds landed near his feet, hopping closer in the hope of crumbs.

"Bread isn't good for you, you know." Dominic extracted some ham from his lunch, tore it into tiny pieces then threw them onto the grass near his feet. It didn't take the birds long to pluck up the courage to grab the handout. Dominic chuckled and threw them a few more scraps. It was a beautiful day. He felt good after a morning's hard work, stretching his muscles and getting his hands dirty. He still had the scent of fresh-mown grass in his nostrils. Best of all, he had his enigmatic, gorgeous boyfriend to go home to. He'd never imagined he could be so contented and at peace.

"Lunch break's over. Time to get back to work. Sorry, guys." Talking to the birds didn't seem weird. He had a whole new perspective on nature since meeting Evrain. He stood, scattering a few crumbs, then downed the last of his juice. Making sure he had all his trash with him, he headed back to the van. On the road toward town, he noticed two women. Their presence wouldn't have attracted his attention but they weren't moving or talking, just staring in his direction, which seemed strange. A few months before and he wouldn't have given it a second thought, but Evrain had taught him to be suspicious and to trust no one. Dominic fingered his pendant. He put his trash in the van, giving the women a chance to move on. When he turned to see if they were still there, they hadn't moved. He stared back at them, then started to walk toward them with purposeful strides. As one, they turned and moved away, taking the first side street they came to. When he got there, there was no sign of them. The scattered houses and array of mature trees provided plenty of cover. They could be hiding anywhere and he didn't have time to go searching for them.

Walking back to his van, Dominic pulled out his cell phone. He called Evrain, giving him a quick description of what had happened.

"I want you to come home, Dominic. Right now."

Dominic rolled his eyes. "Calm down, Evrain. I can't do that. I've got two more clients to see this afternoon and I won't let them down."

Evrain cursed under his breath, just loud enough for Dominic to catch. "What have I told you about obedience?"

Dominic's dick twitched at Evrain's tone. He sighed. "They've gone, Evrain. I'm wearing the star and I'll be careful. Please don't make me come back."

"If I insist, will you do as you're told?"

Dominic shifted his feet. He wanted to say no, that he was a grown man and quite capable of making his own decisions. Deep down, though, he knew he couldn't disobey Evrain. There was silence for a moment then Dominic whispered, "Yes." He could picture the smirk on Evrain's handsome face and shook his head in wry admission of defeat. He pulled his keys from his pocket, expecting to be ordered home, and carried on walking to the van.

"Very well. You can stay." Evrain didn't sound happy. "Ring me after your next job and keep your eyes open." He disconnected without waiting for Dominic's response.

"Wow, I'm being trusted to be a grown-up." Dominic smiled. He knew how hard it must have been for Evrain to grant this concession. He understood his protectiveness. Evrain inhabited a scary world that he was still new to, and Dominic knew he felt guilty about dragging him along.

He'd already suffered at the hands of Symeon Malus. Evrain just wanted to make sure he never had to experience anything like that again. Dominic touched his collar-length hair. He'd been physically altered by an evil warlock. No wonder his lover was paranoid about his safety.

His next job, in the neighboring town, was uneventful. Once he was done, Dominic dutifully made the call Evrain had requested even though nothing had happened. He was beginning to think Evrain's caution was unwarranted. But later, as he was clearing up at the end of his final job mowing a massive lawn the size of a football field, he saw the two women again. They were a little farther away and he had to squint into the sun to see them, but it was definitely the same two people. They just stood and stared at him, not moving.

"Fuck, it's like a scene from *Stepford*," Dominic muttered. As he went to press the speed-dial button on his phone, it started playing *Witch's Promise* by Jethro Tull.

"Evrain." Dominic answered the call.

"They're there again, aren't they?" Evrain's voice was cold and calm, but Dominic caught a hint of something else in his tone—fear.

"How did you know?"

"I felt your anxiety."

Dominic didn't ask how that was possible. "They aren't doing anything, just standing there watching me. I'm coming home now."

"No detours, Dominic. I'll expect you shortly."

"I'm fine, Evrain. I'll be back soon." Dominic disconnected the call. He loaded a few tools into the van, looking nervously over his shoulder. The two women were still there, unmoving but managing to exude an aura of malevolence. He didn't know why he felt that way—they were completely nondescript and had done nothing to suggest they meant him harm—but somehow he knew they did.

* * * *

Evrain gripped the phone so hard the keys pressed indentations into his fingers. He wanted nothing more than to go after Dominic, find him and bring him home. He hated being apart from him but now, when he was in danger once again, the separation was unbearable. Channeling had created an emotional link between them and it was becoming stronger all the time. He could feel when Dominic was happy, when he was sad and most strongly when he was scared. The last made Evrain sick to his stomach but he had a house full of people, one of whom had not been invited.

He'd gone outside to make his call in private but now returned to the cottage kitchen. The room that seemed cozy when it was just him and Dominic became overcrowded with four people around the table. Gregory and Coryn sat at one end. Nathaniel Alberich lounged on one side, his hand clamped around the neck of the unwelcome guest seated next to him.

"Dominic is on his way home. Perhaps now, Damon, you could explain what the hell you're doing here?" Evrain snapped. "Or do you have some kind of death wish?"

Damon cowered in his seat. "Do you think I'd be here if I had any other choice?"

Nathaniel gave him a light cuff to the head, ruffling his hair. "Mind your manners. You're lucky I didn't blast you out of existence."

"I wasn't doing nothing."

"Anything. I wasn't doing *anything*."

"What are you, the grammar cop?"

"No. I'm the warlock who's going to tan your hide if you don't start explaining yourself. I came here for a sociable visit with friends. I didn't expect to have to drag your sorry ass out of the woods, ruining my best pair of Ferragamos in the process." Nathaniel scowled in the direction of his muddy boots.

"Where's your boyfriend gone?" Damon hunched his shoulders.

"Felix is my driver. He's waiting in the car, probably listening to dire country music and snacking on the knucklebones of boys who can't control their mouths."

"Not a boy. Your gorilla hurt me."

"No, he didn't. If he'd wanted to do that, we'd be looking for supplies of O Negative about now. You fell over your own feet then landed face down in a nice soft layer of rotting vegetation. Now, stop avoiding the subject. What are you doing here?"

Evrain listened with interest. A connection already seemed to be developing between Nathaniel and Damon and their interplay was intriguing. He tried to examine Damon objectively. He was slight with dark hair that curled at the ends. His grey eyes were so shadowed they were almost black. There were traces of half-healed bruises on his face and from the stiff way he held himself, Evrain guessed there were more beneath his clothing. He was pretty, in a haunted, waifish kind of way. It was difficult to imagine what Symeon might have done to him.

"How old were you?" Evrain asked. "When…"

"When Symeon sank his claws into me?" Damon dug his teeth into his already-abused lower lip.

Evrain nodded.

"Sixteen. I was with him six years." He shivered. "I'm not here to make excuses but I would like to make up for what I did if I can."

"No one here will hurt you." Evrain gestured for him to continue. "Tempting though it is." He didn't think Damon deserved to be let off too easily. Not yet.

Damon took a deep breath. "Have any of you heard of Imelda Krenick?"

"The self-proclaimed leader of the Octis Coven," Gregory announced. "Nasty bunch."

"Octis Coven?" Evrain had never heard of it, or them.

"Group of power-crazy bitches who give witchcraft a bad

name. The worst kind of self-serving sorority, interested in nothing but furthering their own interests, whether that be wealth, power or influence. All three if they can manage it."

"They sound like a charming bunch," Evrain said.

"And Symeon is working with them." Damon stared, unblinking, at Evrain.

"There can only be one reason for that." Gregory frowned.

"Agreed," Nathaniel narrowed his eyes.

"Perhaps one of you would like to enlighten the rest of us?" Evrain's voice was tinged with sarcasm. That earned him hard looks from both Nathaniel and Gregory. He sighed. "I don't need both of you treating me like a child. I get enough of that already."

"It would be better if we waited for Dominic," said Gregory. "Then we won't have to go through the whole sordid tale twice. I'm sure Damon would prefer not to have to explain himself more than once."

"How do we even know if he's telling the truth?" Evrain glared in Damon's direction. "He's hardly proved himself trustworthy so far."

"I'll know if he lies," Nathaniel stated with certainty. "If he does, he'll regret it."

Damon gulped. He edged his chair a few inches away from Nathaniel, who grinned. Evrain was reminded of a wolf he'd seen at a wildlife park back in Scotland—one who'd just been presented with a bloody carcass. He checked his watch, then his phone in case there were any more messages from Dominic, but there was nothing. His skin itched. He shoved his chair back because pacing had to be better than sitting. The window panes rattled in a sudden squall.

"Control your emotions, Evrain. Dominic will get here as quickly as he can." Gregory tried to soothe him but Evrain didn't want to be pacified. He wanted Dominic in his arms where he belonged.

"You're very fortunate to have found your soulmate, Evrain," Nathaniel said. "I haven't been so lucky yet."

"Oh, I'd assumed that Felix…"

"No." Nathaniel chuckled. "Though he would be amused to hear it."

"So how do you control your power?" Evrain asked. "I could barely manage to light a candle before I was able to channel through Dominic."

"No," Gregory snorted. "He just blew things up."

"I hope you don't mind me asking?" Evrain scowled at his godfather.

"Not at all." Nathaniel drummed his fingers against his thigh. "Over the years, I've learned to filter the energy through multiple people. Unless they are particularly sensitive, they feel nothing because the load is shared, the power spread thinly. It's not perfect. A single channel would be much more effective but it allows me to manage the winds in the way I need."

Evrain was impressed. It must have taken great self-discipline for Nathaniel to manage his power in the way he had.

"I have enough trouble channeling through one person," he admitted.

"Because you love Dominic and you don't want to hurt him?"

"Yes." Small talk could only distract Evrain for so long, however interesting it was. "Where is he, damn it?"

"I'll take a walk down the lane." Coryn stood up. "I'll meet Dominic and explain what's happening. He won't want to walk in on all this unprepared."

"I should go!" Evrain moved toward the door.

"You will not." Gregory banged the table. "Exposing yourself when you're in this mood would be dangerous. You stay put."

Evrain felt like stamping his foot but he caught Nathaniel's knowing smirk. Some of his frustration dissolved as he realized how petulant he was being.

"One of these days I may just have to paddle your behind," Gregory threatened.

Damon giggled. Nathaniel gave Damon's ear a sharp flick. "Quiet, brat."

Evrain shook his head and sighed. "Save your energy for Coryn. I'll behave."

Gregory grunted. "And I just spotted a pig flying past the window. I could use a drink. Show me where the mulling spices are and I'll heat some wine. Agatha always did know how to magic up a good brew."

"At least you didn't suggest a pot of tea," Evrain snarked.

"And I thought you British folk lived on the stuff," Nathaniel said.

"Ninety-nine percent of the population probably couldn't function without it. I'm an anomaly."

"You can say that again," Gregory chuckled.

Nathaniel burst out laughing. Evrain decided that he was outnumbered, outgunned and that silence was the better part of valor.

Chapter Four

Dominic pulled up in his usual spot then put the van in park. He rested his forehead on the steering wheel and took a deep breath, relieved to be home. A tap on the window nearly scared him out of his wits. His heart pounded until he saw that it was Coryn. He opened the door, giving Coryn an embarrassed smile.

"You startled me. I'm afraid Evrain has me a bit spooked."

"Sorry." Coryn gave his shoulder a comforting pat. "I've been waiting for you."

"Why? No, don't tell me. I can imagine." Dominic scrambled out of the van, relieved his legs held him without shaking.

"When he's worrying about you, young Evrain is a major pain in the ass. Gregory almost had to chain him down to stop him driving to your last job to get you."

"Gregory needs a gag spell to use on him."

"Oh, he has one of those." Coryn winked, making Dominic a little more at ease. Coryn had that effect. He exuded calm. "I might have to suggest it."

"What's going on, Coryn?" Dominic asked. "I saw two mildly strange women a couple of times, that's all. Why all the panic? For all I know they might just have a thing for sweaty gardeners."

"For God's sake, don't even suggest something like that to your boyfriend unless you want to kick off the apocalypse. Let's get you back to the cottage before Evrain starts blowing things up. Gregory will explain everything."

Dominic decided it was best not to push Coryn any further. For a while, they strolled along the path to the cottage in companionable silence.

"Is Nathaniel Alberich here yet?" Dominic asked.

"He is. He arrived a while ago and brought a surprise guest with him. He found Damon lurking in the trees."

"What?" Dominic had so many questions but Evrain was waiting at the cottage door, wind whipping his dark hair into disarray. The violent gusts died as soon as he caught sight of Dominic.

"Do you even know where the accelerator pedal is on that bloody van? Does it have some kind of limiter? Or perhaps you stopped to meditate on the properties of oregano."

Dominic looked at the twigs and leaves strewn all over the garden and realized just how agitated Evrain must have been. He opted for diplomacy. "I'm sorry. If I'd known how worried you were, I would have broken all the speed limits and red lights to get back here."

"No, you wouldn't, because that would have been dangerous."

"There's no arguing with you, is there?" Dominic found himself wrapped in strong arms, tight enough that he was going to have bruises. "You have a really strange way of pronouncing oregano. And I've never meditated in my life."

Evrain grunted and hugged him harder.

"Evrain, he's safe." Gregory, sounding impatient, called from the doorway. "For goodness sake, let him go and come inside."

Evrain scowled but released his hold. He kept a proprietary arm around Dominic's shoulders as they went inside and Dominic found he craved the continued contact. The room was saturated with the aroma of mulling wine and for a moment Dominic was distracted as he tried to identify various spices. Then he took in the people seated at the table. He froze.

"I hardly believed Coryn when he told me. What the hell is he doing here?" He stared at Damon, hands clenching into fists. "The last time I saw him, he punched me in the face. He had a chain around my neck. Then he tried to attack Evrain with a knife!" He took a determined step forward. Damon cowered in his seat, lower lip trembling.

"We'll get to that but fuck, you're sexy when you're defending me!" Evrain said, sounding pleased.

"Scary, not sexy," Damon muttered.

"Evrain, perhaps introductions are in order?" Gregory's tone was all reprimand.

Dominic realized that there were other people in the room. His face heated and suddenly the floor was the most fascinating place to look. He was hyperaware of his grass-stained clothes and work-tousled hair. As if sensing his discomfiture, Evrain cupped the nape of his neck and squeezed.

"Dominic, I'd like to introduce Nathaniel Alberich." There was a scrape of wood against stone. Across the table, Nathaniel stood and gave a slight bow. "Nathaniel, this is my partner, Dominic Castine."

"It's an honor to meet you, Dominic."

Nathaniel was a handsome man. He had a similar aura of power to Gregory, holding himself with confident certainty. It seemed all warlocks were cut from the same cloth. He made Dominic feel shy and nervous.

"Um, hi." Dominic managed a brief smile.

Nathaniel nodded as if acknowledging Dominic's suitability as a warlock's partner. Dominic couldn't help but feel he'd just passed some kind of test.

With Evrain's gentle encouragement and a nod from Coryn, Dominic sat at the table, though his seat was a bit too close to Damon for his liking. Gregory ladled spiced wine into goblets then passed them out. Damon clutched his so tightly his knuckles went white. The aroma of nutmeg, cinnamon and wine filled the room, at odds with the atmosphere of dread that seemed to envelop all three warlocks. Dominic sat and waited for the bad news.

"You are both already aware that there are very few powerful warlocks on the planet."

Gregory paused and Dominic wondered at the fact that three of those warlocks were sitting right there in the room with him. The world was a peculiar place, with layers and depths he had never imagined. He focused on Gregory's face and his lips as they moved.

"However, there are considerably more witches. Most are completely benign, with only traces of elemental ability. Some are more powerful—like your grandmother Agatha, Evrain, who was a strong earth witch. None have strength in more than one element—that power is limited to men—and even then they cannot command fire or air. There exists a very small minority who object to that distinction." Gregory sipped his wine. "Over the centuries those few have come together to form a Coven of sorts—though it's insulting to the majority of witches to give it that name—an affiliation of witches with similar dispositions. It's currently known as the Octis Coven."

Dominic swallowed, imagining scenes of bubbling cauldrons and old hags in black pointy hats.

"Forget every preconceived idea you might have about witches, Dominic." Gregory could apparently read minds. "Octis is well financed, technologically adept and highly organized. They always have one plot or another on the go but nothing that has really affected us. This time they've gone too far. Damon here tells us they've joined forces with Symeon Malus."

Evrain snorted. "How can Symeon be of any use to them? We left him virtually powerless."

"One thing members of the Octis Coven can do is brew a good potion. They can probably restore Symeon's strength, if temporarily. As long as he helps them, they will keep him supplied with the tonic he needs to stay strong."

"But why?" Dominic was curious. "What can Symeon do for them that they can't do themselves? Doesn't he represent the very thing they hate?"

"He can battle another warlock." It was Nathaniel who answered rather than Gregory. "It is common knowledge in our world that Gregory and I are allies. Neither of us have ever agreed with Symeon's lust for power. On this continent Symeon is their only option."

"I still don't understand," Dominic said. "Forgive the dense, non-magical one, but why would a bunch of witches want Symeon to fight another warlock? What would they gain?"

"Not *any* other warlock." Nathaniel frowned as he responded. "They will want him to battle Evrain."

Dominic's confusion must have shown on his face. Nathaniel turned his gaze on Evrain. "They are after your blood, Evrain, and I'm afraid I mean that literally."

Beneath the table, Dominic grabbed Evrain's hand and squeezed it.

"A warlock's blood is incredibly potent when it's used in magical spells." Coryn took up the story. "Because you are so powerful and young, Evrain, your blood is a prize worth any partnership, however corrupt. They can't use Symeon's, his power is only temporary. Gregory is too old."

"You're not old!" Dominic protested, directing his gaze to Gregory.

"Old enough," Gregory replied. "I'm not nearly as strong as I used to be."

"And I'm strong," Nathaniel commented. "But only in air and earth. My abilities with fire and water are weak. Evrain, I'm afraid, is a gourmet temptation as far as the Coven is concerned because he is strong in all four elements."

"Please stop talking about me like I'm some kind of snack," Evrain griped.

"Hush." Dominic smacked Evrain's thigh. "Listen."

Damon snickered. Evrain gave him a look that could freeze hellfire and Nathaniel cuffed him.

"Quiet, brat. You haven't earned the right to enjoy yourself at other's expense."

Damon pouted but kept giving Nathaniel sideways glances.

"What can they do?" Evrain asked. "The cottage is warded

well, Agatha made sure of that, and I'm quite capable of defending myself against Symeon. I've proved that once already."

"Don't get cocky, boy," Gregory warned. "We don't know what they'll try, but the fact that they have people watching Dominic is worrying. You both need to be careful and vigilant."

"Where did you get all this information from?" Dominic felt as though he was missing a page or two of the story. Everyone else was a chapter ahead and he was still catching up.

"Damon," Gregory said. "He…"

"Let him tell me." Dominic cut Gregory off. "I want to hear it from him."

Damon's eyes widened. He chewed on a ragged, dirty fingernail. Dominic examined him closely, noting the dark circles beneath his eyes, lank hair and pallid skin. His cheekbones were sharper, as if he'd lost weight and his gaze darted from place to place, never settling anywhere for very long. He couldn't fight the pang of pity that conflicted with his need to consider Damon an enemy.

"Don't let him hit me, okay?" Damon's voice trembled. "And Evrain has to promise not to zap me." He folded his arms.

"You're in no position to argue with anyone, boy." Nathaniel pulled Damon's arms away from his chest then laid them on the table. He encircled one slender wrist with his hand. "Do as you're asked."

"Not a boy." Damon didn't attempt to move his arm. "Fine." He stared at the table rather than at Dominic or Evrain. "I was sixteen when I fell for Symeon. It was a ridiculous crush, but he was so…enigmatic. He hooked me good and lured me in with promises of power and wealth when all he really wanted was a willing body to channel through. I loved him and that was enough for it to work. To him I was a tool and a convenient ass to screw whenever the urge took him."

Dominic shuddered. He'd had experience of Symeon at first hand. He'd witnessed the way Symeon had treated Damon and Damon was right. Any love between them had been one way. Dominic doubted Symeon even had the capacity for love.

"When Evrain defeated Symeon that night...I had no idea what to do. He'd held me in thrall for so long, I'd lost my identity. If I didn't obey him, he hurt me. Sex became punishment. When he took Dominic I hoped he might switch his attention, but you resisted him and he took his anger out on me. I admit, I wanted revenge, so I helped him. Then that night, everything went to hell."

Nathaniel stroked Damon's wrist. "Slow down. Speak clearly. Symeon doesn't control you any longer. You're safe here."

Damon sniffled. He cast a quick, anxious glance at Evrain. "I didn't have anywhere else to go. I went back to the property Symeon used to hold Dominic. He wasn't there and he didn't turn up for a long time. I don't know where he went, but when he did come back I hid from him in the attic then ventured downstairs. I think I could have stood directly in front of him and he wouldn't have noticed. He was obsessed with Evrain, screaming and yelling about what he was going to do to him, but he couldn't even light a candle. His power was utterly depleted."

"Symeon Malus without his power is incredibly dangerous." Gregory massaged his temples. "Because he'll do anything to get it back. Something we should have considered when we left him alive."

"He started making calls. I caught the name Imelda. She leads the Octis Coven, I'm sure of it. He made arrangements to meet with her and when he hung up he was smiling." Damon shuddered. "I never want to see that expression again."

"He got out of the house then made his way here. Nathaniel caught him skulking outside when he arrived earlier," Coryn explained.

"I wasn't skulking," Damon protested. "I was just working out what to say when I knocked on the door. I didn't think I'd be welcomed with open arms."

Evrain wiggled his fingers and Damon shied away. His chair tipped backward but Nathaniel righted it before he could fall.

"Stop that, Evrain," Dominic admonished. "It took courage to come here, even if it was self-serving."

"I don't have anywhere left to go," Damon reiterated. "I have no money and no friends. I relied on Symeon for everything, he made sure of that." He wiped his nose on the back of his hand.

"Forewarned is forearmed," Evrain said. "But I'm still not convinced these people are as dangerous as you all seem to think they are."

"If Symeon catches you unawares, Evrain, with Octis boosting his power, he could block you. Not permanently, but long enough to overpower you." Gregory steepled his fingers. "You're not invincible. None of us are."

Nathaniel nodded. "It's true. Believe me, if the Octis Coven gets hold of you those bitches won't be happy with just one vial of blood. You'll become their source of wealth and they'll never let you go."

"Well, that's...depressing." Evrain sighed. "There's nothing we can do this evening, so what happens next?"

"I think Coryn and I will return to our hotel," Gregory announced. "Nathaniel, perhaps you would care to join us for dinner? We can discuss our options for keeping Dominic and Evrain safe." He pushed his chair back.

"Don't you think that's something we should be involved in?" Evrain asked.

"No. You and Dominic can take common sense precautions. We need to consider the bigger picture. There may be leverage we can utilize."

Nathaniel nodded. "Agreed. Felix is probably spitting nails by now, sitting out in the car. A meal with agreeable company is just what we need."

"Um, what about him?" Dominic gestured at Damon.

"He'll be coming with me," Nathaniel said decisively. "I need a new project."

"Hey! I'm not a project," Damon complained. "What if I don't want to come with you?"

"You are badly in need of a spanking," Nathaniel declared. "Something I'll be only too happy to administer here and now if you don't do what you're told. Or perhaps you'd enjoy displaying your bare ass while I turn it pink?"

Damon gaped. "I don't... You can't..."

"Move it, boy, or I'll leash your dick and drag you out of here."

Damon licked his lips, eyes wide.

"I think he quite likes that idea," Dominic muttered to no one in particular. "Are all you warlocks Doms?"

Coryn gave his shoulder a light squeeze. "Yes, they are. Which means they need us to keep them under control." He grinned. "They like to think they're in charge, but we know better. Mind you, I think even Nathaniel will have his hands full with Damon. That young man's submissive streak doesn't seem that wide to me."

"Oh, I think he'll cope." Dominic watched Nathaniel herd Damon toward the door. "He's probably just what Damon needs."

"They'll be good for each other, I think." Coryn gave Dominic a hug. "Look after each other, Dominic. Don't allow Evrain to underestimate the danger you're both in."

"I won't."

Dominic and Evrain said their goodbyes and everyone left with a promise to be back within the next couple of days. Dominic tried to quell his sense of anxiety. If this problem could get two experienced warlocks riled up it wasn't something he could just forget.

Chapter Five

Evrain closed the door behind them and whispered a few words over the lock. "An ant won't get through there now, I've fused all the metal." He turned and gave Dominic a speculative leer. "Now, what on earth are we going to do with what's left of the evening?" He flickered his fingers and flames ignited in the hearth, casting an orange glow across the rug.

"Nothing, before I have a shower!" Dominic grimaced, "I've been working all day, remember?"

"Mmm. I love it when you smell of the earth. Makes me want to do wicked things to you."

"You want that whether I'm clean or dirty."

"True."

"But it's been a really long day. I want a hot shower, then food, then sleep. I don't want to think about warring witches and warlocks until tomorrow and I can't believe I'm saying that."

Evrain opened his arms and Dominic walked into them. "I'm sorry, love. Your world has been turned on its head, hasn't it?"

"Yours has too." Dominic snuggled against Evrain's body, absorbing his warmth.

"Yes. But when Agatha told me I was a warlock, everything fell into place for me. It was a like a fog had lifted and I could finally see the real world. You had everything you thought was real ripped away."

"But I got you." Dominic gazed into Evrain's strange green-gold eyes. "Makes all the freaky shit worthwhile. I just don't want you hurt."

"It's my job to protect you, not the other way around. And 'freaky shit'? You are so overdue a spanking."

Dominic's cock twitched. "You wish."

"I do. But I'll allow you to shower first. You can prep for me while you're up there. Unless you'd like me to come along and do that for you?"

"No!" Dominic needed a few minutes of alone-time, not just for getting clean but also to get his scattered thoughts in order.

Evrain pouted, but then his cell rang. He cursed and Dominic took his chance to escape upstairs to the bathroom. He just heard the words "Hi, Mum…" before the noise of cascading water drowned out the sound of Evrain's voice. Dominic pulled the bathroom door closed. He stripped off his dirty clothing, leaving the discarded items in a heap on the floor, then climbed beneath the spray with a contented sigh.

Laughing at his mother's latest news on the antics of his younger sisters, Evrain kept his eyes on the stairs. He could hear the water running and his head was filled with images of Dominic, naked and wet, rubbing gel over his smooth skin. Talking to his mother while sporting an iron-hard erection was not a habit he wanted to get into. At least he didn't have to talk much. He paced the room, contributing to the conversation when he could get a word in. His mum was threatening to visit if he didn't keep in touch more often. He said all the right things, made promises to call or email every week and appropriate excuses about being busy with his job. She seemed content with his answers and he hoped she wouldn't be hopping on a plane anytime soon. He loved his family but the last thing he needed was more people he cared about getting in the line of fire. He needed to be able to focus his attention on keeping Dominic safe.

Evrain set about pulling together a simple meal. Of the two of them, Dominic was the far better cook, but Evrain could manage the basics. There was fresh local salmon in the fridge, so he mixed some breadcrumbs with chopped parsley and Parmesan for a crust. Baked potatoes and broccoli would complete the meal. He put the potatoes in the oven first. With any luck, he would have time to give Dominic a spanking before they were ready. That thought made him smile as he finished preparing the fish and vegetables. With everything ready to go, Evrain adjusted the furniture to his liking. He wanted Dominic over his knees and needed a chair without arms for the best position so he moved one across from the kitchen area. Next he took a log from the wood basket. Focusing his power, he manipulated the material into a smoothly fashioned plug. He ran his hands over the silky grain, ensuring there were no rough edges. It was large enough to stretch Dominic's channel but not so big as to cause pain. Evrain set a pot of his home-made lube next to the fire to warm. Now all he needed was Dominic.

"Are you nearly done up there?" Evrain yelled up the stairs. The bathroom door clicked open.

"What are you shouting about?" Dominic's pained voice came back to him. "And why are you channeling?"

"Don't bother dressing. I have plans for you." Evrain visualized Dominic standing there dripping, a scowl on his handsome face. Dominic enjoyed being ordered around — he just wasn't that good at admitting it.

"Damn it, Evrain. Give me five minutes."

Evrain listened to footsteps heading for the bedroom. He was confident Dominic would do as he was told. He took the seat next to the fire and made sure the new toy and lube were within reach. While he waited for Dominic he thought about the events of the day. Against his expectation, he had liked Nathaniel Alberich. The man was blunt, but his eyes sparkled with good humor and shrewd intelligence. He would make a valuable ally. Evrain could understand why Nathaniel and Gregory got on so well. They were formed from the same mold. He suspected that both of them saw him as an arrogant, inexperienced boy who needed some discipline drummed into him. Much as he hated to admit it, they were probably right. He wasn't so stupid as to think he knew better than they did, with their years of experience, not when Dominic's safety might depend on his willingness to learn.

Damon was another matter. He had sympathy for his position. He'd been abused for a long time by Symeon Malus and deserved a break. Nathaniel might be just the man to provide it, though he didn't imagine Nathaniel would go too easy on Damon. He chuckled. It seemed warlocks were all alike in some ways.

"What are you so amused about?"

Evrain turned to see Dominic standing at the bottom of the stairs, a towel wrapped around his narrow hips. He'd dried his hair to just damp and it hung around his shoulders. For a moment, Evrain's mind blanked as lust consumed him. He shook his head. Dominic had more power over him than another warlock ever would.

"I was thinking about how Nathaniel Alberich will handle Damon."

A slight smile traced Dominic's lips. "I imagine...firmly. He didn't seem the type to take any crap from anyone."

"Something we have in common." Evrain beckoned him over. "Come here, sweetheart." The firelight danced in Dominic's eyes but he didn't move. Evrain watched as his lover took in the setup by the hearth. His eyes widened when he spotted the plug.

"You've been busy." He swallowed and his Adam's apple bobbed. "Is that why you were channeling?"

"Yes. Just a little handicraft. Gregory keeps telling me I need to finesse my skills — I might as well make something functional while I'm at it. Why don't you come over here and take a closer look?" Dominic was hardly a skittish colt to entice with gentle words but he was stubborn. He wouldn't do anything he didn't want to.

Dominic gave an exaggerated sigh then walked the few

paces to Evrain's side. Evrain stood to face him.

"You won't be able to resist me for long." Evrain stepped into Dominic's personal space. There was little more than a finger-width between them. Dominic's breath smelled of mint and his body of herbal shower gel. He leaned in for a kiss. Just a gentle brush of lips. Dominic swayed toward him with a soft moan. Evrain ran his hand down the curve of Dominic's back and when he felt the edge of the towel, he pulled it away.

"Mmm. That's better." Evrain followed the swell of firm muscle with his fingertips. "Your ass is a work of art." He cupped one round cheek, enjoying the smooth skin. "Your skin is cool. Is it warm enough in here for you?"

Dominic's answer was to lean in for another kiss. "Stop talking, Evrain."

This time the joining of their lips was fierce. Dominic was just as demanding as Evrain, who found he had to battle for dominance. He nibbled Dominic's plump lower lip and, at the same time, pushed the tip of a finger into his hole. The heat inside him was intense. Evrain pulled him closer, wanting Dominic to know how hard he was, how much he made him want him. He sank his finger a little deeper. Dominic rose on his toes.

"Stop teasing me." He reached behind his body, grabbed Evrain's wrist then tried to force him deeper. He rubbed his rigid cock against Evrain's cloth-covered bulge. "Need you."

"You'll have me. When I decide." Evrain withdrew his finger. He gave Dominic's backside a light slap. "You are badly in need of discipline." He sat on the chair, patting his thighs. "Over my lap."

Dominic stood there, flushed and gorgeous, his cock standing to attention.

"Don't pretend you don't want it. Your body betrays you." Evrain waited patiently for Dominic to submit. The war between need and resistance played itself out on Dominic's face until he worried his swollen lip with his teeth and took a step forward. Evrain could not have found the words to describe his deep satisfaction when Dominic draped himself across his lap, but warmth filled him. He made an effort to control his emotions as flames leapt up the chimney.

"Please don't singe my ass," Dominic muttered.

Evrain just held back a snort of laughter. "It's definitely going to get hotter, but no burns, I promise." He brought his cupped palm down on Dominic's unmarked skin.

"Ow!" Dominic wriggled but pushed his ass up as if begging for more.

"I know what you're doing." Evrain parted his thighs to prevent Dominic from gaining friction against his cock. "You get to come when I say so, not before." He rained a few more hard smacks against Dominic's exposed flesh, admiring the pink glow that resulted. He judged Dominic's moan was more about frustration than pain. Using consistent force, he focused his efforts on the crease between ass and thigh for a while. Dominic's breath hitched. His muscles tensed.

"Oh no you don't!" Evrain twisted his fingers, sending a coil of air around Dominic's dick. He made it rotate at the base of Dominic's balls, teasing and constricting at the same time. "So much more fun than a cock ring, don't you think?"

Dominic panted and groaned simultaneously. Evrain resumed the spanking until Dominic relaxed, his muscles becoming pliant. Evrain guessed he had reached that place where pain disappeared and became erotic pleasure. His breathing was slower and deeper. He no longer twitched beneath the blows.

Evrain reached for the wooden plug and the jar of lubricant. He slathered the toy with a thick layer of the viscous substance then pressed it firmly against Dominic's hole. Dominic was so relaxed that the plug slid home with little resistance. Evrain gave it a nudge or two and released the collar of air preventing Dominic's ability to come. He encouraged Dominic to move so that he was sitting in his lap rather than splayed over it. He held him close, applying light strokes to his cock.

"You've done so well, sweetheart. I can feel the heat from your ass against my thigh. So warm. You deserve a reward."

Dominic rocked a little, applying pressure to the plug. He sighed then his head fell forward onto Evrain's shoulder as he came. Evrain took a deep breath as Dominic's unique scent filled the air. Sticky warmth coated his palm. Dominic shuddered. He made the sweetest sounds while his body tensed through the aftershocks of orgasm. Evrain's smile was one of pure satisfaction. Controlling Dominic's pleasure made him feel more powerful than any use of his gift. His dick ached but that in itself was a turn-on. He could wait for his own release. After they ate and Dominic had had a chance to recover, Evrain had every intention of pounding his lover's well-spanked ass until he screamed.

"I need another shower."

Evrain smiled. Dominic was coming out of sub-space with a rumbling stomach and some attitude.

"No, you don't. I haven't finished with you yet. Once we've eaten I intend to have my wicked way with you."

"You put something in my ass."

"I did." Evrain chuckled. "Does it feel good?"

"Full." Dominic wriggled. "How did I get in your lap?"

"Does it matter?" Stroking Dominic's back had him purring with pleasure. "I'd put some balm on your ass, but I want you to feel everything all through dinner. I want you desperate and begging for me before we get to dessert."

"I'll go dress."

"I don't think so. I prefer you naked."

"S'not fair. You have clothes on."

"Mmm. Delicious, isn't it?"

"Want to see you."

"Later. You won't appreciate my cooking if you're distracted."

Dominic pouted. A lock of dark copper hair fell across his face. He shoved it away. "Why do I put up with you?"

"Because you love me," Evrain said with certainty. "And you get off on me telling you what to do."

Dominic wrinkled his nose but didn't deny it.

"So go sit at the table and I'll feed you."

"Then fuck me?" There was an appeal in Dominic's voice.

"Definitely."

Dominic slipped from Evrain's lap then ambled across to the table. He took a seat, sucking in his breath as his no doubt tender ass hit the chair. He sent Evrain a baleful glance.

"What?" Evrain tried for innocence but came up short.

"Sadist." Dominic poured himself a glass of water.

Evrain made his way to the stove. Once the salmon and vegetables were cooking he joined Dominic at the table.

"The food won't be long. I didn't want to cook the fish until we were ready. Dry salmon is against the laws of nature." He cut a couple of slices of nutty granary loaf then slathered them with butter. "Here, this will keep you going." He put one slice on a plate then slid it across to Dominic, who devoured it before Evrain had even taken a bite from his own slice. He held that one out to Dominic. "Here, you need it more than I do."

"I'm hungry."

"I can see that." Evrain gave Dominic an indulgent smile.

"Hey, I worked hard today then sat in a room full of warlocks and listened to all the bad things that people are planning to do to you. Then you…you…wore me out even more." Dominic's cheeks flushed with color.

"I know. I guess we react differently to these situations."

"You thrive on it, don't you?"

Evrain couldn't deny he did get something of a thrill out of the unusual and unexpected. He nodded. "While you prefer the certainty of things that grow."

"Plant a seed, it does what comes naturally. No surprises. No magic required."

"Aren't we just like a seed? We're growing together. Me into my power, you into a role that makes it possible."

"That's very profound—and oddly surreal considering I'm sitting here naked."

"It's a good look on you." Evrain got up. He dished up the food then returned to the table with laden plates. He put his down then circled behind Dominic to put the other one in front of him. He placed his hands on Dominic's bare shoulders, stroking him with light touches. "Eat. Build up your energy. I want to put that nakedness to good use."

Evrain was quite pleased with his culinary efforts. The fish was light and flaky, the vegetables firm and the potatoes fluffy inside. He also had Dominic to stare at across the table. All in all, it was a very satisfactory meal. Dominic glanced at him every now and again from beneath his thick copper lashes. The blush didn't fade from his cheeks.

Evrain finished his food first. He pushed his chair back a little to stretch out his legs. He thought about the smooth wooden plug nestled inside Dominic's body.

"What are you grinning about?" Dominic asked as he finished his final forkful of broccoli. "You look like you're about to do something I'm going to regret."

Evrain pinched his thumb and forefinger together. Visualizing what he wanted to achieve, he drew them slowly apart. Dominic's eyes widened and his lips parted.

"What are you...? Evrain! Stop that."

"Just making the plug a little bigger." Evrain repeated the motion with his fingers.

Dominic stood, the movement so abrupt his chair fell over, landing with a crash.

"Oh God!" Dominic panted. He reached behind his back.

"It won't come out, love. Not until I remove it. I'd say it's pushing on your prostate quite nicely." Evrain admired the tensing of Dominic's muscles and the light sheen of moisture making his skin shine. His erection was a thing of beauty. He grabbed the edge of the table, steadying himself.

"Please!"

Evrain couldn't resist the plea. He maneuvered Dominic away from the table and into his arms. He ran his fingers down Dominic's spine and over the curve of his ass until he found the base of the plug. Just the slightest pressure elicited a half-scream from his lover. "I've got you." He turned Dominic around so that he could press against his back. He gave his cock a couple of tugs, spreading the warm bead of pre-cum over its head until it glistened. Dominic whimpered and begged, his words barely coherent. Evrain held him steady with an arm around his waist then used his free hand to undo his own pants. He released his aching cock with relief then eased the plug from Dominic's channel. As it was pulled free, Dominic moaned.

"Just making room for me, sweetheart." Evrain tested Dominic's readiness with a finger. "Still nice and slick." He pushed into him with a single smooth thrust. Much as he would have liked to demonstrate the kind of control it took to hold off, he couldn't. A bit of graceless, not quite gentle, shoving and Dominic was able to brace himself against the wall. "That's better. More resistance." Evrain jerked his hips. "You were made just for me. You know that?"

"Less conversation, more action, witch-boy." Dominic pushed his ass back.

"If you can still talk, I'm not doing this right." Evrain proceeded to render Dominic speechless. Close to the edge, he managed to get one hand around Dominic's cock, the other around his throat. The soft heat surrounding his dick needed no magical enhancement. Dominic used his inner muscles to squeeze him hard.

"Pushy bottom." Evrain responded with a few punishing thrusts. He twisted his fingers around Dominic's straining shaft. "You can…"

Dominic didn't wait for him to complete the sentence. His spine arched. He pressed his butt against Evrain's groin, sealing them together. His orgasm sent tremors through his body and he moaned in ecstasy. Feeling the intensity of Dominic's release ignited Evrain's body. His fingers closed around Dominic's throat. Dominic pushed against his touch as if inviting him to grip harder. The sense of absolute power over another human being gave Evrain such a head rush that he lost all coordination. His gliding thrusts faltered and he came in a series of awkward jerks.

As the euphoria faded he regained enough awareness to loosen his grip. He slipped from Dominic's body then turned him around, drawing him into a close embrace.

"I love you." His voice trembled. He traced the finger-shaped marks on Dominic's neck. "I crave you."

Dominic pushed him away a few inches.

"And you bewitch me."

Evrain stared at him. "I can't believe you said that with a straight face."

Dominic dissolved into laughter. "You crave me? Really? Have you been reading trashy romance novels?"

Evrain tumbled into one of the armchairs next to the fire, pulling Dominic with him.

"I'm serious! You're an addiction. You're in my blood. In my bones." He fingered the cord around Dominic's neck. The stone star was warm where it had been in contact with Dominic's skin. "I should fit this to a leather collar."

"In your dreams!" Dominic squirmed, trying to escape. Evrain just held him tighter.

"Indeed. That kind of thing features in my dreams almost every night." He leered, making Dominic laugh even more.

"Then take me to bed. It's about time I got *you* naked."

Evrain didn't have to consider that suggestion for long.

Chapter Six

It had been almost three weeks since the gathering at the cottage. Returning a couple of days after the initial get together, Nathaniel and Gregory had declared their decision to let matters lie for a while. They needed to draw Symeon out. Give him enough rope to hang himself, or at least to trip over and fall on his face.

Evrain mulled this over as he lay in bed resisting the need to get up. He still wasn't comfortable being used as bait. If it had just been him he'd have been all for it, but Dominic was a different matter. He wanted Dominic safe. He sighed. He had to travel to the office so abandoning the soft warmth of his bed was mandatory.

"Stop thinking so much and get up," Dominic mumbled.

Evrain gave him a quick smack on the behind but swung his legs out of bed. He dressed quickly then headed downstairs. Dominic, clad in just his jeans, padded after him.

"The warm weather does have some advantages." Evrain leered at his boyfriend. "Shame I don't have time to take full advantage." He glanced toward the door from his seat at the kitchen table. He frowned then shook his head. "Must be imagining things." He went back to reading the detailed brief spread in front of him on the table.

"Imagining what?" Dominic strolled over carrying two glasses of freshly squeezed orange juice. He put one in front of Evrain.

"Thought I heard scratching at the door. We probably have mice."

Dominic sipped his juice. He cocked his head to one side.

"Can't hear anything."

As if to give the lie to his words, there was a loud scrabbling at the door.

"I heard that."

"Can't be dangerous, the wards haven't been disturbed."

"So you want me to take a look?" Dominic fiddled with the star pendant nestled in the hollow of his throat.

"I suppose so. I don't sense any danger." Evrain continued reading. "I have to get through all this before I head in to the office. Should have done it last night but you distracted me." Evrain grinned at Dominic's affronted stare.

"You know, I'll be glad when Gregory's back to resume your training. I seem to recall reminding you last night about that brief. I ended up gagged and tied to the bed."

"You were talking too much," Evrain said. He closed his eyes, picturing the image of Dominic, lean limbs spread, strapped down for his pleasure.

"You… You… Oh, I give up." Dominic marched over to the door. He yanked it open, then stood there for a moment.

Curious, Evrain craned to see. "What is it?"

Dominic took a step back. "It's for you."

Holding back a sigh, Evrain shoved his chair back then walked over to the door. Sitting front and center on the step was a fat, long-haired black cat. He stared at the animal. The cat stared back, bright green eyes unblinking.

"I thought witch's cats were supposed to be lean and slinky," Dominic commented. "This one has been scoffing too many mice. And it has more fluff than a woolly mammoth."

The cat turned its gaze on Dominic, managing to come across as mortally wounded.

"I'm a warlock, not a witch," Evrain muttered. "And how do you know it's here for me? Probably just wandered away from its owners."

"You don't believe that for a minute. How many cats show up at a front door then scratch to be let in?"

"So why is it just sitting there?"

"Perhaps it's waiting to be invited inside and I can't believe I just said that." Dominic went back to the kitchen table. He sat then sipped his juice.

"Do you want to come in?" Evrain asked the cat, which sashayed past him into the cottage. "Fuck, I'm talking to an animal as if it's human. I'm losing it." He shut the door. The cat paused, licked a paw then leapt into one of the armchairs next to the fireplace, curled up then closed its eyes. Purring, loud enough to shake the foundations, started up.

At a loss, Evrain turned to Dominic.

"Don't look at me. Seems like we've acquired a new housemate." Dominic shrugged.

"But where did it come from? I grew up with dogs. I have no idea how to take care of a cat."

"I imagine it's fairly self-sufficient. Can't say I've much experience with supernatural animals either—and I'm assuming that this one isn't anywhere close to being normal. I like cats, though."

He might have imagined it but Evrain thought the purring grew even louder. "She might not stay."

"How do you know she's a she?" Dominic asked.

"Oh…I don't. She feels like a female."

Dominic gave him a quizzical look.

Exasperated, Evrain shrugged. "I can sense it. She's… content."

"You're vacuuming up her fluff when she sheds everywhere."

"You're being very accommodating," Evrain said.

"Why fight it? Even I get the feeling she's going nowhere. There must be a reason for her being here and she wouldn't have made it across your wards if she presented any danger. She's cute."

Evrain examined the pile of dark fur ensconced in his favorite chair. "Then I suppose we'd better give her a name." The cat opened one eye. An ear twitched.

"What do warlocks' cats normally get called?"

Evrain could tell that Dominic was holding back a laugh.

"How the hell should I know?" He tried to get a sense of identity from the cat. "I don't think she has a name yet."

"Well, she's black—how about Sooty?" An indignant yowl came from the chair. "Maybe not."

"Hmm, what about Shadow?" Evrain approached the cat. He stroked its soft head. "What do you think about that? Suitably mysterious?" The cat butted his hand. "Seems like that meets with approval." More loud purrs answered him.

"Good to know someone has control over you." Dominic chuckled. "She's been here less than five minutes and you're already her obedient slave."

"You want to spend the next week in chastity?"

Shadow rolled onto her back. She began to groom herself as if losing all interest in the conversation.

"You'll have to buy cat food while you're in town today." Dominic ignored the threat that was more of a promise. "And she'll need grooming every day with all that fur, so pick up a brush too."

Evrain checked his watch. "Damn! I need to go. You're working here today, aren't you?"

"Yes." Dominic nodded. "Don't worry, I'll keep an eye on the fur ball. There's probably a tin of tuna in the cupboard. That will keep her going for a while. Perhaps I should think about planting some catnip."

"You think this is all highly amusing, don't you?" Evrain grabbed his car keys.

"Sure do."

"Enjoy yourself while you can. Check out the gates of hell on the internet. It's time you had a lesson in mythology."

Evrain gathered up his paperwork then headed for the door.

He sauntered along the lane, taking his time despite the cool mist, which was thick enough that he couldn't see far into the trees on either side of the path. The usual lines of the trunks were smudged like a charcoal drawing, the edges softened and blurred. It appealed to his designer's eye. *Three weeks and nothing's happened. Perhaps Octis have decided we're not worth the effort.* Dominic had been working with his regular clients and hadn't seen any more strange women lurking or watching him. Evrain worked from home some days but still went to the office several times a week and he hadn't seen anything suspicious either. He shrugged. The status quo suited him just fine for now. If the biggest adventure of the week was having a peculiar, overweight cat show up at his door, so be it. *Must give Gregory a call about that later. I don't remember him saying anything about pushy felines.* There was plenty to be said for domestic harmony, especially with Dominic to get home to.

He hummed as he walked, planning a trip to a great toyshop he had discovered in Portland that stocked some unusual bespoke items. Dominic was probably researching the gates of hell on the internet already. Knowing him he'd be wondering why Evrain had an interest in Rodin's sculpture or one of the various places around the world depicted as an entranceway to hell. Evrain's actual interest lay in a particular set of evil steel rings that he wanted to see around Dominic's pretty cock.

Juggling his phone, papers and keys, Evrain staggered then fell as a metaphysical hammer slammed into his senses. He clutched at his head, pain stabbing into his skull. He reached for his power but found nothing but impenetrable blackness. Through knives stabbing the back of his eyeballs, he registered that he'd been blocked. He fought back the wave of panic threatening to consume him but it was hard to breathe. The blackness closed in.

Moisture seeping through his clothes was the first thing Evrain became aware of. The cold penetrated at his hip and along one arm. His hair was wet and twigs dug into his cheek. It took him a few moments to work out where he was. He was still on the path between the cottage and his car. With an effort he got to his knees, though weakness threatened to send him head first into the dirt once more. Casting around, he could see no sign of either his keys or his phone. His papers were a scattered, soggy mess on the path. He swallowed, trying to get some moisture back into his mouth, which was dry as dust. There was some kind of restriction around his throat. Tentatively he brought his fingers up to touch and found a metal collar locked around his neck. He tugged at it, succeeding only in making deep grooves in his fingertips. He couldn't see it to identify what metal it was made of but he guessed it was something pure enough to maintain the block on his power, because when he reached for the elements he felt nothing.

"You fucking idiot!" He couldn't believe how complacent and careless he'd been. He spent so much time nagging Dominic about being careful to the point of paranoia yet had failed to even keep a cursory eye out for danger himself. Self-flagellation was pointless. He needed to focus because Symeon Malus had to be close. The question was, why was Evrain alone on the path when Symeon could easily have transported him somewhere while he was unconscious? What kind of sadistic game was Symeon playing?

A rustling in the trees attracted Evrain's attention. Through the mist, which he now guessed might not be natural, he could make out two glowing red points of light. He glanced around. There was no way he was leading anyone or any*thing* back to the cottage. More red spots appeared through the gloom and he could make out the rough outlines of large doglike shapes. There was a snarl. Leaves shivered. It seemed Symeon wasn't satisfied with a straightforward victory. All Evrain could think about was Dominic and how vulnerable he was back at the cottage. Symeon had been there before. He knew where it was. Evrain had to get as far away as possible.

He staggered to his feet, shaking his head in an attempt to clear his vision. He pivoted then ran into the trees on the opposite side of the path. He had no idea where he was going, just that it had to be in the opposite direction to the cottage. He had to make sure that Dominic stayed safe. His leg muscles ached as he twisted and turned amongst the trees, ducking the groping branches, leaping over knotted roots set to trip him. The mist seemed to thicken but perhaps it was just his eyesight blurring. Then he went down as a stabbing pain clawed at his thigh. He ignored the hot wetness of his blood and ran again, as fast as he was able.

His feet sank into a thick layer of mulch. Clumps of mud and sodden leaves kicked up from his heels at every step. His lungs heaved with the effort of running. Lurching to a halt, he placed a hand on the nearest, moss-clad trunk and tried to listen across the pounding thump of his heartbeat. Nothing. He took a few desperate, ragged breaths. He had no illusions that his pursuers had given up the chase. A hungry howl in the distance confirmed what he already knew.

Evrain debated the point of running on. Symeon and his wolves, or whatever they were, would catch up to him sooner or later. His legs were already burning and the warm stickiness of the wound in his thigh would provide a nicely scented trail. Dominic's face filled his mind. He had to keep running for as long as he could. The mist dissipated and instead heavy rain came down in a deluge, adding to his misery.

"Just great." Evrain pushed sweat-dampened hair out of his eyes. "Perfect." He ran. He could hear his pursuers closing in, howls splitting the air. He stumbled to a halt again, catching the gleam of red eyes to one side and then the other. There was nowhere left to go. He backed against a tree, though it afforded little protection. He might be beaten but Symeon would not find him groveling on his knees in the mud. He squared his shoulders and closed his eyes, picturing the beautiful face of his lover, dark red waves framing creamy skin, soft lips and bright blue eyes. It was too late for regrets. He blinked. Eyes burned malevolent crimson in the murk. A hand grasped his shoulder, long black nails sinking into his flesh through the fabric of his saturated shirt. It took all his courage not to cringe as a smooth, gloating voice whispered in his ear,

"Finally, Evrain, we meet again. You cannot imagine how much I have looked forward to this moment."

"Fuck you, Symeon." Evrain shook off the other warlock's hand. "What was this game of hide and seek all about?"

"You made things too easy for me. I didn't want to deny myself the joy of the hunt. Especially with such…delicious prey." Symeon raked a long nail down Evrain's cheek, leaving a burning line in its wake.

"Only you could be so desperate as to sell your soul to the Octis Coven." Symeon's eyes narrowed. Evrain laughed. "Yes, we know what you're up to."

"And yet here you are with my collar around your neck, blocked from your power."

"You're impotent, Symeon—I saw to that, remember? Whatever those bitches are feeding you will wear off and when your power fades, I'll be ready. You're pathetic."

Red lightning danced around Symeon's hand. "Watch your tongue, boy, there's no one here to help you this time. Be nice to me or I'm going to hurt you in ways your limited mind couldn't even begin to imagine."

"At least my mind isn't clouded by hate, Symeon. You see no further than your own need for revenge. When the bitches have what they want they will discard you like the trash you are."

"You arrogant little shit!"

Flashes of red light stabbed into Evrain's body. He convulsed with pain, falling to his knees. Symeon grabbed his hair and pulled his head back. "When Octis is done with you, you're mine, Evrain, and I can't wait to make you suffer. And when you are all used up, I'll be going after that sweet redhead of yours. He and I have unfinished business."

"I let you off lightly last time, you psychopath. I won't be so considerate again."

Symeon raised his hand. Evrain could do nothing to avoid the blow and a brief flash of red was followed by darkness.

Chapter Seven

Felix leaned against the counter in Nathaniel's kitchen, the solid Italian marble pressing into his lower back. Nathaniel watched him, waiting for him to speak.

"Come on. I know you can't wait to tell me what an idiot I am." He scrubbed a hand through his hair.

"Seems like you already know." Felix raised his glass of iced water in a mocking toast.

Nathaniel fixated on the slice of lemon floating in his own glass. "There's something about him. I don't know what it is."

"He's a brat."

"Probably."

"Definitely. You're not seeing that side of him yet because Symeon Malus no doubt beat the spirit out of him. A few weeks knowing that he's not going to be smacked around or used for what his body can provide and he'll revert to type. Class A brat."

"How do you get over six years of abuse?" Nathaniel twirled the ice in his glass with his finger.

"You have to remember that Damon was a willing participant — at least to start with. He loved Symeon. Well... he was infatuated with him. He's only realized recently that the way Symeon treated him wasn't normal for a Dom-sub relationship."

"Symeon is a piece of shit. As warlocks we have even more responsibility to take care of those we love. The power takes control to a whole new level. Damon did not consent to be used like he was."

"And yet Symeon was able to channel through him. There

had to be love involved."

"I think Damon genuinely cared for Symeon. He was too young and naïve to recognize Symeon for the sadist he is. That man wouldn't know love if it smacked him on the nose with a rolled up newspaper."

Felix snorted. "If Symeon can get what he needs from the Octis Coven, he won't be bothered about hunting Damon down."

"He'll be safe with us." Nathaniel rolled his shoulders, listening to his joints pop. "I'm more concerned about convincing him to stay."

"You want him."

It wasn't a question and Nathaniel couldn't deny it. Damon was exactly his type. "Yes."

Felix shook his head. "That boy has trouble written all over him. I suggest you invest in some sturdy handcuffs and a leash."

Nathaniel blinked.

"Ah, you already have them, I suppose?"

"It's always good to be prepared." Nathaniel grinned. "Damon's been moping around the house for two weeks now. He's drifting. Time to take him in hand."

"Good luck with that." Felix's expression was dubious. "If you want him productively employed, I'm intending to clean out the garage this afternoon. I could use some help."

"You could eat off the floor in there," Nathaniel commented.

"Which is why it needs scrubbing to keep it that way."

Nathaniel wasn't going to argue. The cars and garages were Felix's domain. It was more than his life was worth to interfere with either. Felix gave him a brief wave before disappearing to his world of crankshafts and carburetors. Nathaniel set his glass next to the sink then set off to find his house guest.

He had installed Damon in one of several large guestrooms, one with its own attached bathroom. Damon hadn't ventured out very much. He showed up on time to eat. He seemed clean and tidy—helped by the few clothes and toiletries Felix had supplied—but there was an air of melancholy about him. Nathaniel tapped on Damon's door but didn't wait for a response before entering. Damon was lying on his bed wearing a pair of faded jeans and a snug black T-shirt. His feet were bare and his dark hair needed combing. He scrambled from the bed, face bleaching white.

"I...I'm sorry, Sir." Damon's voice shook.

"Sorry for what?" Nathaniel asked. "I'm not aware that you have anything to apologize for."

"I just... You don't seem to want me around. I'll leave as soon as I pack. Not that I've got anything to put my things in." He glanced around the room, seeming panicked.

"You don't get away from me that easily," Nathaniel said. "I apologize. I thought giving you some space for a while would help you settle in and clearly I've achieved the opposite."

"I'm not used to having my own room, Sir. Symeon made me sleep at the foot of his bed, unless he wanted... Well, unless he..."

Nathaniel held up a hand. "No need to explain. You're quite safe here. No one is going to make you do anything you don't consent to. I won't invade your room again without your invitation."

"It's your house, Sir." Damon stared at his bare toes.

"Yours too, while you stay here. You're free to leave at any time, Damon, but I would prefer that you stay. I think I can give you what you need, if you'll allow it."

"I've not had choices before, Sir. I find things easier if someone tells me what to do."

"That's not at all surprising for a natural submissive. You should still be involved in decisions made on your behalf. I think it might be helpful if we drew up a contract. One we both agree to." Nathaniel didn't attempt to get any closer to Damon, much as he wanted to hold him and provide some comfort. "It helps that you know what I am. Being a warlock is not a simple thing to explain to a prospective partner."

Damon's face flushed a pretty shade of rose. "You don't hate me, Sir?"

"I don't know you, but I'd like to. I have a feeling we'll be compatible and I'd like to explore that, if you're willing."

"Yes! I mean, I think I'd like that too."

Nathaniel hid a smile. Damon was transparent as crystal. "Very well. Then let's go downstairs, make ourselves comfortable and have a chat about what it is you need." Nathaniel pinned Damon with a stern look. "Don't bother with shoes and take your shirt off."

Damon's pupils dilated until black almost covered the dark gray of his irises. Nathaniel headed for the stairs, not checking if Damon did as he'd been ordered. It was quite clear to him that the boy needed to be taken care of — the craving for affection shone in his pretty eyes.

Nathaniel chose a corner of his huge sectional couch where Damon could elect to sit next to him or keep some space between them. He stretched out his legs, crossing them at the ankles. Damon hesitated at the door then padded across the room. He paused in front of Nathaniel then sank gracefully to his knees.

"I'm impressed, Damon, but for now you can sit on the couch. Until we have a proper agreement between us, I'm your host, not your Master." Damon rose then perched on the edge of the couch. Tension was apparent in every taut muscle. "I didn't ask you to come down here shirtless because I wanted a chance to ogle. You've been moving stiffly and I wanted to check for injuries."

"I'm fine," Damon muttered, folding his arms across his chest.

"You're bruised." Nathaniel could see the remains of old wounds on several areas of Damon's torso. He wondered how much more was hidden elsewhere. "Symeon beat you." Damon didn't respond, but then Nathaniel hadn't asked a question. "Any contract between us is going to be founded on honesty. Tell me right now if anything he did is still bothering you."

"Not now, Sir. He... He wasn't careful the last time he took me. He liked it rough."

"I'm going to need to take a look, Damon. Stand up then drop your pants."

Damon's sigh was one of resignation rather than resistance. His pants slipped over hips that were a shade too thin. Faded yellow finger-shaped bruising was apparent on both sides of his body. There were traces of old welts on his buttocks.

"Show me."

Damon bent, reached back and pulled his ass cheeks apart. Nathaniel didn't touch. "There's still some reddened skin, but I can see you've been taking care of yourself. I would like my doctor to give you an internal examination though. Okay, you can pull up your pants."

"Like what you see?" Damon's attempt at bravado fell flat.

"You're too thin. You've been abused. But you do have a cute ass. Thank you for cooperating. My intent was not to humiliate you. If we reach an agreement, then I will require access to your body at all times. Before you ask, that doesn't mean I'm going to fuck you. Your health and wellbeing will become my responsibility. Have you ever taken drugs?"

Damon finished fastening his pants. "No, Sir. Symeon didn't allow alcohol or drugs, not even cigarettes."

Nathaniel grunted. "That's probably the only thing he would be able to claim as a similarity with me. I expect you to keep your body clean and healthy, inside and out."

"But you're not going to fuck me? You don't want me?"

"I don't believe I said that. But it won't happen until you ask for it."

"My choice?"

"Always." Nathaniel ran a hand through his hair, a repetitive habit he realized he needed to break. "I propose we begin with a simple contract that outlines a few rules. This is for you just as much as me, so I expect you to contribute." He grabbed a pad from a side table then took a pen from his shirt pocket. "I have few requirements. Honesty, obedience and a willingness to learn. I would like to give you some responsibilities around the house and Felix may also have tasks for you. You'll follow an exercise regime and support me in my work."

"Symeon mentioned you worked with the winds," Damon stated. "I don't know much more than that."

"I have the strongest connection with the air element. My business is in renewable energy — wind farms mainly, though not exclusively. My abilities mean I am able to ensure their maximum efficiency. A large percentage of the organization's profits is plowed back into research."

"But you don't have anyone to channel through? No boyfriend?"

"No. I have learned to channel through many people at once. It's not as effective and it's hard work, but it does the job."

"Maybe one day you could channel through me?" Damon suggested.

"Perhaps, but in the meantime you can support me on my trips to manage the winds. Felix has been plaguing me to find an assistant for a while."

"I want to be useful. I'll help in any way I can."

Damon seemed pleased. Nathaniel wrote a few lines on his pad, summarizing what they'd discussed so far.

"What happens if I break any of your rules, Sir?"

"They're our rules, Damon, not just mine. Break them and you'll be punished."

"By you?"

"By me. In a way I will explain to you at the time. Any punishment will fit the crime." He grinned. Damon rolled his eyes.

"Doms. Always ready to hand out a spanking."

"I think you'd enjoy that too much for it to be considered a punishment."

"I'm not saying a word."

"Probably best. Now is there anything you want to add to the sheet?"

Damon took the pad and pen. He hesitated before writing a line or two then handed it back to Nathaniel.

"Nathaniel will protect Damon from Symeon Malus and all other supernatural threats," Nathaniel read. "I'll certainly do my best." He laid his hand on Damon's knee. "I promise." Damon didn't move his leg.

* * * *

That evening, Nathaniel, Felix and Damon settled around the kitchen table to share a meal that Damon had prepared. The room was filled with savory aromas and Nathaniel found his mouth watering. Damon, still barefoot but now wearing a T-shirt with his jeans, had a smudge of flour on his nose. He placed a bowl of salad on the table, which was already set for three.

"This actually smells great," Felix announced, sounding surprised. "It's a big improvement on anything you've ever produced, Nate, and I haven't even tasted it yet."

Nathaniel shrugged. Felix was right. Neither of them could cook worth a damn. They kept half the restaurants in the area in business with their takeout orders. "I'm amazed Damon even found enough ingredients to cook with."

"The contents of your fridge are pathetic," Damon said, cheerfully. "Good thing I'm a miracle worker. I will need to go to the market, though, if you want me to carry on with catering duty." He placed a steaming dish on the table. "I made shepherd's pie. There was ground beef in the freezer and some frozen vegetables and I found some potatoes that were just about salvageable. It would be much better with more fresh stuff." He distributed three warm plates then handed Nathaniel a serving spoon. Nathaniel gave it back.

"You should do the honors."

Damon's cheeks pinked but he set to ladling generous portions onto each plate.

"Oh my God, this is good," Felix managed between mouthfuls. "Chain him to something in here, Nate. He should never be allowed to leave the kitchen."

Damon giggled. The sound made Nathaniel smile. *Damon's young – he should be enjoying himself. He hasn't had much to smile about for the last few years, that's certain.*

"But if I can't go out for groceries, you won't get to eat more home-cooked food, Felix."

"I'll take you myself. I'll even push the cart." Felix shoved another forkful of food into his mouth with an orgasmic moan.

"You can go shopping, Damon," Nathaniel said. "But I don't want you going out alone until we know what Symeon is up to."

"Yes, Sir."

"No arguments?" Nathaniel was somewhat surprised that Damon didn't balk at being guarded.

"I know Symeon too well, Sir. I'm a useful possession. He won't want to lose me." He nibbled on his lower lip before resuming his meal.

A few minutes later all the plates were empty. Damon made coffee after stacking the dishes by the sink. Nathaniel sipped his, enjoying the slight bitterness on his tongue.

"Take a seat, Damon. I'd like you to tell us about how you first met Evrain and Dominic. If I'm to support them, I need to know as much as possible about what happened. Gregory told me about the fight between Evrain and Symeon but I don't know much about how that point was reached."

"I'm not very proud of what I did, Sir. My part in what happened wasn't nice." Damon stared at the well-scrubbed table.

"It's history. You were under the influence of evil. You weren't to blame, Damon, and I'm sure Evrain realizes that."

"He wants to fry me. Or turn me into a slug."

Felix snorted. "Sorry."

Nathaniel glared at him. "Not helping, Felix. While Evrain

could certainly achieve the first option, he couldn't manage the second, so no need to have nightmares about waking up with a craving for lettuce. He knows I've given you my protection so there will be no frying anyone either."

"Okay, well, it all started when Evrain came into his power. Symeon was furious because Evrain is many times more powerful than he is. He went to visit him. Tried to get him to agree to an alliance."

"But Evrain is honest," Nathaniel interjected. "He was brought up, at least in part, by Gregory and Agatha. They would have made sure his path was straight."

"Yes," Damon agreed. "Evrain would have nothing to do with him. Symeon became obsessed. He wanted to crush Evrain and he realized that the easiest way to get to him was through Dominic. He set up a work appointment for Dominic then when he was driving home, I ran him off the road." Damon chewed on a nail until Nathaniel pulled his hand away from his mouth.

"It's okay. Carry on."

"Symeon kept Dominic prisoner at a property he owned. Dominic tried to escape and Symeon hurt him. He changed him. Made him even better looking than he already was. He wanted Evrain to see what he could do. He wanted him to feel helpless." Damon shuddered and half sobbed. "He got Evrain to agree to meet him. They fought and…you know the rest."

"Thank you, Damon. That can't have been easy."

"I wasn't kind to Dominic while he was a prisoner. I was jealous. Symeon gave him more attention than me, then used me to channel while he changed him." Tears rolled down his cheeks. "I'm as bad as Symeon."

Nathaniel had no doubt that Damon's remorse was genuine. He could sense the guilt and regret. "You could never be as bad as that snake, Damon. Evrain and Dominic won't hold a grudge. You can make amends by never getting anywhere near Symeon ever again. Without you to channel through, his power is reduced. He's reliant on the Octis Coven's potions—not a very secure place to be. Once they get what they need from him, the Coven will drop Symeon faster than Felix can consume a Snickers bar."

"And that's fast," Felix contributed.

"He couldn't channel through me now anyway," Damon muttered. "I don't love him. I don't feel anything for him. I'm just numb." He peeked from beneath thick, black lashes.

"Nobody here is going to tell you how you should be feeling. I'll avoid too many platitudes because I can't know what's going through your head, but time will help. You can talk to me anytime."

"Or me," Felix said. "For what it's worth, but only if you feed me." Felix's grin was disarming.

"You're already a step ahead of me. I've never had that offer." Nathaniel glared at Felix.

"You talk my ears off every time we're in the car. I should be paid as your personal therapist, not just your driver," Felix complained.

Damon's moved his head from side to side as if watching a tennis match. "You two are...certifiable."

"Welcome to the family." Nathaniel and Felix clinked their coffee mugs together in a toast.

Chapter Eight

Dominic stepped from the shower, wrapped a towel around his hips then wiped a broad swath of condensation from the mirror. He still found it hard to accept the reflection as his. He blinked, holding back a sigh. For weeks after his rescue from Symeon he had reached automatically for a razor every morning, but his face, and the rest of his body, had remained stubbornly hair free. Only his copper mane, eyebrows and lashes remained. He actually missed shaving and that was something he'd never thought would happen. He had tried to cut his hair a few times, hacking at the shoulder length waves, but within an hour it had grown back.

Evrain rarely mentioned it, but Dominic knew that he liked the changes Symeon had wrought even though he hated that Symeon had had his hands anywhere near Dominic. The visual results appealed to him but he was conflicted about it. Dominic wasn't sure how he felt about that. He toweled his hair roughly and glared at his reflection. "I look like a fucking girl!" Symeon's magic had smoothed the angular planes of Dominic's face, given him a perfect complexion and thickened his lashes. His eyes were a more startling color, his hair like silk.

"It's just a face. It doesn't matter." Dominic didn't want Symeon in his head. If he allowed that, Symeon had won. He needed to accept the changes and forget how they had happened. Self-pity wasn't helpful.

The things Gregory had said on his last visit were frightening. Dominic felt so powerless in this strange world of warlocks and witchcraft. On the surface at least, Evrain seemed to embrace it with ease. Dominic detested the thought that his boyfriend could be in danger just because of what he was. He was also afraid that if Evrain were attacked, there would be little he could do to help him.

He cleaned his teeth, hung up his damp towel then ambled naked into the bedroom to find some clean work clothes. It was a shame Evrain had already left. He had a habit of waiting for Dominic to dress after a shower then stripping him slowly. He'd nuzzle Dominic's cock then reward him with a slow, torturous blow job, keeping him hovering on the edge of release as long as possible.

Dominic had no problem being on the on the other side of that particular equation. He chuckled at the thought and rummaged through the small selection of garments in his wardrobe. He wasn't seeing customers so he went for comfort, choosing a pair of worn jeans with rips across one thigh and a soft navy T-shirt, the design so faded it was indiscernible. It was warm enough to go without socks but he didn't want to get blisters from his heavy work boots, so found a pair that weren't too thick then pulled them on.

Finally, he raked a comb through his hair more roughly than he needed to. It still got tangled but there was nothing he could do to alter the style. Sighing, he walked to the window to pull the curtains open. It was a bit murky outside.

Wow, weather sure changes fast around here. He'd been hoping for a dry, sunny day in the garden but now it looked like rain might set in. He froze, grasping the edge of the fabric, straining to see through the thick mist. Just visible behind the gate at the end of the narrow garden path were the dark outlines of two figures. He stared, trying to make out who was there but there wasn't enough visibility to ascertain any details. He had a terrible feeling that the shapes were of the two women who had been stalking him a few weeks back.

"Shit!" He yanked the thick drapes closed then ran for the stairs, a cold fist closed around his heart. His phone was lying on the kitchen table. He grabbed it then speed dialed Evrain but the phone went straight to voicemail.

"Surely he didn't forget to connect his phone in the car?" Even as he muttered the words Dominic knew that it was unlikely. Evrain preferred to be connected at all times. He had a hands free kit and always used it. "Perhaps he's on another call." Dominic made sure the front door was bolted, then tried the phone again. There was still no reply. In the chair next to the fire, Shadow stirred. Dominic crouched down beside her. "What's going on, puss? I have a bad feeling about this, how about you?" The cat gave her paw an idle lick. "I'll feed you then give Evrain another try." Dominic needed to do something to keep himself calm. He found a can of tuna at the back of a cupboard and an old china dish to put it in. As soon as he started using the can opener Shadow evacuated her seat, stalked across the room then proceeded to wind around his ankles in a way that would probably void his medical insurance. "All right! It's coming." A head butt to his calf prompted him to move faster. He placed the dish on the floor then added another filled with water. "There you go." Shadow ignored him, head buried in the food amid enthusiastic slurping noises.

Pushing back the urge to keep calling Evrain, Dominic trotted back up the stairs to take a peek through the bedroom curtains. He couldn't see the garden gate from anywhere else in the house. The rain was teeming down now, obscuring his view, but he could still make out the two figures standing there, unmoving. He sat on the edge of the bed staring at his phone. He hadn't left Evrain a message but the missed calls would be showing up. Evrain always got in touch when he saw the notifications. He was paranoid about Dominic's safety.

"Shame he's so careless about his own," Dominic muttered. His fear was making him angry. He dialed once more just to get the same recording. This time he left a brief message. "Evrain, please call me as soon as you get this... and answer your damned phone!" The hard knot in his stomach would not go away. He went back downstairs then, for a moment, gazed unseeing around the room. Shadow was still immersed in her food bowl. The rain was battering the windows. A cold draft from somewhere caressed his neck. It reminded him of Evrain using the air to tease him.

"Damn it all to hell." Dominic dialed Gregory's number. His heart was pounding and he made a conscious effort to stay calm as the call connected.

"Hello?"

Dominic felt calmer as he heard Coryn's voice. "Coryn, thank God you're there. It's Dominic…"

"Dominic? Hold on, lad, slow down, I'll put you on speaker so Gregory can hear too."

There was a moment's crackling, then Gregory came on the line. "Okay, Dominic, we're both here. Tell us what's happened."

Dominic wished he could sound half as calm as Gregory. "That's just it, I don't know. I'm at home. Those two women are back—just outside the gate. Evrain went to work less than hour ago but I haven't been able to get hold of him. His phone just goes to voicemail. I have a really bad feeling and I don't know what to do…" He trailed off miserably.

"Think, is there anything else you saw or heard?" Gregory's voice came back, sharp with worry.

Dominic took a few deep breaths. "Evrain had to go into the office today so we got up quite early. We were having breakfast when there was a scratching at the door. Evrain answered it because the wards hadn't been disturbed and there was a cat sitting there. She's made herself at home— Evrain didn't seem at all bothered by her."

"Wait—describe the animal."

"Fat, black and hairy," Dominic said. "Seems way too intelligent for a cat, but I'm guessing the supernatural is involved somehow. Evrain barely blinked, just accepted that we have a new houseguest."

"Okay. Continue."

"Evrain went off to work. I went upstairs to take a shower.

I'd dressed and was opening the bedroom curtains when I spotted the two women. They haven't attempted to cross the wards. They're just standing there. They give me the creeps."

"Give me a minute while I call Nathaniel. He's closer than we are and may have felt something. Stay by the phone." Gregory hung up and Dominic paced up and down waiting for him to call back. He had a horrible feeling that every minute lost was a minute that Evrain might not have. When the phone rang again he pounced on it and pressed the receiver to his ear.

"Nathaniel did feel something. He described it as a bit of a jolt. I suspect that Evrain might have been blocked and he agrees that it's a possibility."

"No! That's bad, isn't it? What do I do? I should go out to look for him…"

"No, absolutely not. Stay put. Coryn and I are on the way. I'm going to ask Nathaniel if he can help too but it will take us all a while to reach you." Gregory paused. "I mean it, Dominic. You stay in the house until we get there. Putting yourself in danger is not going to help Evrain."

"Okay, if I have to." Dominic understood where Evrain got his authoritative nature from—Gregory sounded remarkably similar. "But I can't sit here doing nothing. What can I do to help?"

"This is going to sound strange, but I suggest you listen to that cat."

Before Dominic could even think of a response, Gregory hung up. He realized his mouth was open so he shut it, grinding his teeth in frustration. He stared suspiciously at Shadow, but the fur ball was lapping at her water dish, no doubt washing down the immense quantity of tuna she'd just hoovered up.

Dominic wasn't used to feeling so helpless. Although he took a submissive role in his relationship with Evrain he was still an independent person and the feeling of uselessness hurt him deeply. After some unproductive pacing he climbed back up the stairs. He took yet another peek through a crack in the curtains. He could still make out the vague shapes of the two strange women hovering just beyond the garden gate. *What the hell do they want?* He flicked the curtains closed again and sat on the edge of the bed, determined that their presence would not stop him from thinking clearly — Evrain's life might depend on it. Sitting around was getting him nowhere. *I'm going to ask them what they want. They can't get to me through the wards.* Gregory wouldn't be impressed but he wasn't the one with a missing boyfriend.

Decision made, Dominic ran back downstairs. He pulled on his work boots then headed for the front door only to find his path blocked by a cat. Those green eyes were unsettling and too similar to Evrain's. Dominic stared at Shadow. The cat stared right back. It was Dominic who blinked first.

"You can't stop me going out there," Dominic muttered. "And why the heck am I talking to a cat?" He took a step forward. Shadow hissed then bared a fang. "Who knew a ball of fur could be so threatening?" Dominic chuckled, taking another step. Several points of fire ignited in his calf as Shadow sank a few claws into him.

"Hey! What was that for?" Dominic rubbed at his leg. "You don't want me to go out there?" Shadow meowed in a way that Dominic translated as *'of course not, dumb ass'*. "Do you work for Gregory?" Another disdainful half-yowl followed that comment. "Fine." Dominic accepted that he was never going to get past the cat without losing a limb. He took off his boots and that seemed to mollify the animal. He got purrs and a few head butts. Disheartened, he sat at the kitchen table. It would be several hours before either Gregory and Coryn, or Nathaniel arrived. He couldn't just sit doing nothing.

Shadow jumped onto the table, brushing against him to get his attention. Dominic watched as the cat leapt from surface to surface, ending up at the bookcase where she sat, waiting.

"I can't believe I'm letting myself be ordered around by a cat. I get enough of this from Evrain." Dominic pushed his chair back then wandered across to the bookcase. "You want me to read something?" He touched each volume on the top shelf in turn. There were a mixture of Agatha's books and few of his that he'd collected. The subjects were mainly plants and herbs, a few recipe books. He noted they needed a dust. Shadow tapped his finger with a paw, mercifully with talons sheathed. Dominic stopped then pulled it from the shelf. "*Herb Lore & Magery*. Don't think I've ever read this one." He blew dust from the spine. "Looks really old." He took it across to one of the armchairs next to the fire. The fire wasn't lit but even with the rain still hammering down outside, the room wasn't chilled. He sat and Shadow immediately jumped into his lap, kneaded his thighs for a while then collapsed in a contented, purring heap. Dominic shook his head. He was worried. Scared. Reading and stroking the cat might help take his mind off it for a short while.

The day passed at a crawl. Dominic stayed away from the windows, remaining by the fire, which he had lit for something to do. Outside the rain had slowed to a drizzle then stopped. The sun managed to break through the remaining clouds but there was little warmth in it and the inside of the cottage, with its thick stone walls, became chilled. Dominic hoisted a complaining Shadow from his lap then banked the fire. The cat immediately found a spot on the rug to stretch out on, stomach bared to the flames.

"You're going to be a roasted cat if you stay there," Dominic felt obliged to warn Shadow. The gaze he got in response was one of utter contempt. "Fine. But don't come running to me when you singe your fur." He made a mug of hot chocolate but didn't bother with food because he had no appetite. He settled back in his chair. The herb lore book was absorbing even if he didn't know what use reading it would be. He sighed. It shouldn't be too much longer before the cavalry got to him.

The first indication Dominic had that either Gregory or Nathaniel had arrived was the terrifying sound of a violent crack of lightning. It was all the more shocking because the weather was still fine and as far as Dominic knew there had been no sign of a storm gathering. He was usually sensitive to the building pressure of thunderclouds but he hadn't noted any change.

He got up slowly before making his way to the front door. Shadow didn't try to stop him, which he took as a positive sign. He unlatched the door, opening it just a crack, wincing at the creak the hinges made. He was rewarded with the sight of a spectacular light show. The sky, darkened to a bruised purple, was being split asunder by fork after fork of vivid silver lightning. The ground seemed to vibrate with the noise and Dominic hesitated before opening the door a little wider. Each time the sky lit up he could see silhouettes of figures moving in the lane. The scene played out in front of his startled eyes as if a strobe light were suspended above the combatants. He caught intermittent glimpses of the action but never enough to truly determine what was going on. Curiosity overruled common sense as he stared at the staccato picture in front of him and he took a step outside. He could well imagine Gregory berating him for not staying within the relative safety of the cottage, but it was actually Coryn that reached him first, bundling him roughly back through the door and shoving it closed behind them.

"You young idiot! Are you trying to get yourself killed? One stray bolt and you would be fried like an overdone sausage, then Gregory and I would be equally roasted when Evrain got hold of us. I don't think he would appreciate coming home to a charred boyfriend." Coryn softened his words with a firm hug.

"Sorry," Dominic felt obliged to apologize. "But you have to admit it was a spectacular show. It was hard to look away. What exactly is going on out there?"

"The two witches parked outside your gate proved to be a

little stubborn. Gregory decided that some fireworks might persuade them to move, but they seem to be under some kind of compulsion spell to remain and he has had to resort to more persuasive tactics. Nathaniel is assisting."

"What exactly do you mean by more persuasive?"

Coryn grinned in a way that reminded Dominic of wolves he'd seen on television documentaries. It wasn't a pleasant smile and it made him shiver inside. "Gregory is very happy when he gets to employ brute force once in a while. He is usually restricted to work that requires more finesse. He says these brutal jobs keep his warlock muscles toned."

"Is he channeling right now?" Dominic asked.

"Oh, yes," Coryn replied.

"You don't seem to experience much discomfort."

"After all our years together, I barely notice anymore."

"I think I'm jealous." Dominic shivered. "I can only imagine what that kind of force involves. What is he up to?"

"He's doing something to turn the compulsion in our favor. In layman's terms it's like stretching an elastic band too far. The spell will snap back into their minds and have a reverse effect so they will want to be anywhere but here."

The sounds of a furious wind whipped around the cottage like a banshee in full voice, so loud that Dominic had to cover his ears. Then, just as suddenly as it had started, the wind ceased. The silence that followed was eerie and Dominic found that he was holding his breath, until the door opened and Gregory appeared around it with a grin. Nathaniel followed close on his heels. He had a similar expression on his face.

"That was fun." Gregory's eyes sparkled with mischief and Coryn shook his head in resignation.

"You two look like a pair of misbehaving schoolboys," said Coryn.

Dominic wouldn't have dared say such a thing. He hid his smile.

"You know you aren't here to enjoy yourselves, don't

you?" Coryn scolded. "We are supposed to be working out how we can help Evrain."

"I know, I know," Gregory admitted. "But every now and again it feels good to flex the magical muscles."

"It sure does," Nathaniel agreed.

Dominic switched his gaze from one warlock to the other. "Thank you all for coming... I think. The more I see of warlocks in action, the more I realize just how out of my depth I am in this world of yours."

Gregory smiled, more gently this time. "Sorry, lad, I got a bit carried away. Nathaniel and I don't get the chance to work together very often. I haven't forgotten why we're here, I promise."

Shadow wandered across the room, sat at Gregory's feet then yowled at him. "It seems someone else is keen to remind me of my duty." Gregory leaned down then scooped up the cat. "Wow, you're...well fed." Shadow tapped him with a paw, claws sheathed, then settled into his arms, purring with more decibels than could possibly be natural.

"She likes you," Dominic said, somewhat surprised. "She's been acting like my prison guard all day. Wouldn't let me out the door."

"Quite right too. I told you to listen to her, didn't I?"

Dominic gave him a quizzical look. "What aren't you telling me?"

"Nothing." Gregory affected innocence. Both Nathaniel and Coryn gave snorts of disbelief. Dominic decided to leave it. He had other things on his mind, or rather another person.

"Evrain. He's in trouble, isn't he? I gave up listening to his voicemail."

There was a metallic clatter as Nathaniel threw something onto the table. "We found his phone at the end of the lane along with his keys. His car is still there, untouched as far as I can see. Felix would be better able to tell if it has been tampered with."

Dominic fought back nausea. "He's not here?"

"No. We separated at the airport. He and Damon have another task to take care of."

"So Evrain was taken before he even made it to the car?"

"Yes, it seems so," Coryn replied. "There are signs that he ran from something. He headed north into the woods. Drawing whatever it was away from Hornbeam. Away from you."

Dominic's eyes burned. "So what can we do? It must have been Symeon that took him, working with the Octis Coven, I assume. But you don't know where they've taken him?"

"Oh, I think we have a pretty good idea," Gregory reassured him. "Between us, Nathaniel and I have significant resources. We have traced all the buildings that Octis members either own or have an interest in. Felix and Damon are checking out a few addresses in Portland. We don't think they'll have gone any further than that. Portland is their stronghold."

"Gregory, put that cat down. I'll brew some coffee. We have plans to make." Coryn winked at Dominic.

"Yes, my love." Gregory rolled his eyes but took a seat at the table. He did keep Shadow on his lap. "We need to get our heads together and come up with some kind of a plan. Now that Nathaniel and I have removed your little witch problem we can start thinking logically about the bigger one."

"Will they come back? The witches, I mean." Dominic shivered.

"Almost definitely. In fact we're relying on it."

Dominic tried not to come across as bewildered as he felt.

"Stop talking in riddles, love," Coryn said. "Dominic has enough on his mind without you getting all mysterious."

Nathaniel chuckled. Gregory scowled at Coryn, but his eyes were soft with affection. "Yes, dear." Shadow heaved herself up, turned in a few circles then thumped down into Gregory's lap again. "Coryn and I were discussing the possible options for what we could do on the journey here and we've come up with an idea. Nathaniel agrees as well. It's not just a case of finding a way to rescue Evrain now. We need to work out a longer-term solution. Just getting him back isn't enough — the Coven bitches will keep coming after him while his blood is of value to them. We have to find a way to take the temptation away from them."

Dominic couldn't imagine how that was ever going to happen. He just wanted Evrain back in one piece.

Coryn brought a tray laden with mugs across to the table. He distributed coffee then produced a package of cookies. "I brought these from home."

Dominic's stomach growled. He hadn't eaten since breakfast so he took one of the cookies. He forced himself to eat even though it tasted like ashes in his mouth.

"What the Octis Coven values is Evrain's blood, which is a potent ingredient in many spells used by those who have little genuine power," Gregory explained. "We need to contaminate his blood in such a way that it does not harm him but becomes useless for their magical purposes."

"Sounds logical," Dominic said, "but how on earth do you contaminate someone's blood? It must be dangerous."

"Dominic." Nathaniel drummed his fingers on the table. "What can you tell me about the herb agrimony?"

Dominic had no idea what that had to do with anything but Nathaniel's expression was so intense he answered anyway. "I've been reading about it recently." He eyed Shadow with suspicion. "It's a deep green plant covered with soft hair and has a slightly aromatic scent a little like apricots. It's quite common and can be found in most parts of the U.S. — I know there's plenty of it in the fields around here because Agatha kept a supply. It can be crushed for its oil or brewed as a tea and it has a reputation for…purifying the blood. Oh."

Smiling, Nathaniel nodded. "Ironically, witches often used agrimony in their spells and to ward off hexes. When placed in a sachet and hung in the home, it's said to provide protection against goblins, evil spirits and poisoning."

"And we can use this herb somehow, to help Evrain?" Dominic grabbed the small seed of hope with both hands.

"We believe that agrimony, whilst causing no harm to Evrain, will affect his blood in such a way that if the Coven attempts to use it, their spells will be corrupted and no longer work. If he then drinks it regularly, after a few months his blood will be tainted so much that he will not be worth the chase and they will switch their attention elsewhere."

Dominic frowned. "That's all very well, but how the hell are we going to get agrimony into him at all? We don't even know where he is and if what you say about the Coven is true he will be well hidden and guarded. They are hardly going to allow us close enough to let him swallow something."

Nathaniel's eyes narrowed. "There is one thing they need which may allow us to get close enough." He looked worried. "It's a huge risk and Evrain won't thank us for it, but we really can't see another way."

Dominic looked anxiously from Nathaniel to Gregory then to Coryn. "One of you needs to tell me, for goodness sake. I'm not made of glass. I'm not going to break." Thoughts swirled in his head, then it dawned on him. "Oh. Fuck."

Gregory sighed. "The thing they most need in addition to Evrain himself is you, Dominic. His blood is only of use to them if they can extract it while he's channeling and for that they need you."

Dominic thought he might throw up the cookie he'd just eaten. As if sensing his emotions, Shadow jumped onto the table then padded across to him. Automatically he stroked her soft, midnight fur. "Could this day get any worse?"

"I'm afraid so." Gregory frowned. "They need you to be close to him and they have to give him a reason to use his power. Evrain knows that the last thing he must do for them is channel—however, if you are being threatened or hurt there is little that anyone would be able to do to stop him. He certainly wouldn't be able to stop himself. His instincts would take over."

"But surely Octis will realize that we're planning something if I just fall conveniently into their hands?" Dominic didn't like the idea of being anywhere close to a bunch of witches but he would do anything to get Evrain back.

"Indeed, and that is why we must make it as difficult as we can for them to capture you, but not impossible." Gregory steepled his fingers, looking thoughtful.

Dominic kept stroking Shadow, who seemed to know that her function as a stress reliever was required.

"It's to our advantage that the Coven is making use of Symeon Malus because he's driven by his need for the potion they must be supplying him with. Symeon is less likely to suspect that anything is wrong. He'd grab the opportunity to take you without even thinking about it. We just need to make it seem as if we have made a mistake and left you vulnerable."

Gregory leaned forward. He pulled the star-shaped pendant from beneath Dominic's shirt. He closed his eyes, running his fingers across the stone. When he opened his eyes again they glowed briefly.

"Evrain certainly didn't mess around when he imbued the star with protective properties. He's added significantly to what I could do and he put a lot of love into it. It's an extremely powerful defense against witchcraft. If you were without it, Symeon would be able to sense the void left by its absence." Gregory smiled. "I think I know how we can make this work. Symeon will expect us to move you somewhere where we can protect you better. We can make it seem as if we are doing just that, but when we leave, once we are a good way down the lane, you can make out that you have forgotten something important. He will be watching, that I can guarantee. I can ensure that your pendant becomes undone and falls to the ground before you reach the protection of the cottage wards. It will only give him a fraction of an instant to act but I think he will take his chance."

"I'll do what I have to," Dominic said. "Of course I will, but it all sounds risky. How can you be sure Symeon will do what you think he will?"

"I know him, Dominic. He's driven by his own lust for power."

Dominic shrugged. He didn't know enough to disagree. Nathaniel and Gregory had decades of experience in dealing with Symeon.

"When he takes you, you will have to fight him as much as you're able. Shout and struggle as if you are in a panic, afraid. It's a slim chance but I think that his addiction to power will override logical analysis of the situation."

"I don't think seeming afraid will be much of a problem," Dominic stated, his tone wry. "The whole idea of this is terrifying. You know what Symeon did to me the last time he had me. He hates Evrain and he knows that the easiest way to hurt him is through me. I'm Evrain's biggest vulnerability."

"The Coven has too much control over Symeon for him to be able to do anything stupid. Octis will want you in one piece. It will be in his interest to get you to them undamaged."

"And what about Damon?" Dominic asked.

"What about him?"

Dominic thought Nathaniel sounded a shade defensive. "I just mean… Well, won't Symeon want him back? They were together a while. He might believe that Damon still loves him enough that he could channel through him."

"The only feelings Damon has left for Symeon are hate and regret," Nathaniel said with absolute certainty. "He suffered more than anyone at Symeon's hands. It just took him a while to recognize the abuse for what it was."

A glance passed between Gregory and Nathaniel. Dominic knew there was something he wasn't being told but he didn't have the energy to press for information he was unlikely to get.

"Dominic does have a point though," Coryn commented. "Damon could be in danger. Symeon is the kind of man who wouldn't want to lose what he considers to be his property. If he had any clue that Damon had turned to us for help, he'd want to kill him."

Dominic shivered. He wouldn't want to be in Damon's shoes. "I hope he's okay." He meant it and that surprised him a bit. Coryn leaned across the table. He gave Dominic's shoulder a gentle squeeze.

"At least we know he'll be of little interest to the witches — he has no power of his own and Symeon uses him as a tool, nothing more. Felix will keep a very close eye on him, as will Nathaniel."

"Okay." Dominic didn't miss the suggestion that Nathaniel had more than a passing interest in Damon. He chuckled. "I'm glad." He fixed his gaze on Nathaniel, who blushed just a little. "We should invite him to join our club, Coryn."

Coryn nodded. "He'd be an asset."

"What club is this? And I know I'm going to regret the question," Nathaniel asked.

"Support group for the long-suffering life partners of dommy warlocks," Coryn replied with a chuckle. "Membership is very selective."

Nathaniel shot a panicked look at Gregory. "They're ganging up on us!"

"You want to try and stop them?" Gregory shrugged. "Best to just go with the flow. Your life will be a whole lot easier." Gregory sipped his coffee reflectively. "I don't deny this plan of ours is going to be unpleasant for you, Dominic. It's a great deal to ask, but I can see no other way."

"I don't care what Symeon, or the Octis Coven, do to me if it means we can save Evrain. I just want him back, so tell me what I need to do."

"Fine. It's getting late."

Shadow yowled her agreement then retreated to the armchair next to the fire with a green-eyed stare at Gregory.

Gregory flicked his fingers, sparking the wood in the hearth into a renewed blaze. Dominic could have sworn the cat nodded before settling into the chair.

"Do you have what you need to brew some agrimony into a strong tea?" Gregory asked.

"Sure. I think there's some dried leaves in the herb cupboard. I just need to steep it in boiling water for an hour or two. It's a fairly potent herb so it won't take too long. But even if I can get near Evrain, how will I be able to smuggle him a drink?"

"I think we'll need to be a little more subtle than that." Gregory smiled. "You go ahead and brew that tea. Let me worry about how to get it into Evrain. In the meantime, would you mind heading into town and finding some takeout, Nathaniel? Coryn can go with you."

It told Dominic a lot that Gregory would entrust Nathaniel with Coryn's safety.

"Sure." Nathaniel pushed his chair back then stood. "We'll do a bit of scouting around at the same time. Check to see if there's anyone, or anything, lurking in the undergrowth." He licked his lips as if relishing the idea of finding something. Or maybe it was just the anticipation of food.

Chapter Nine

Evrain's first awareness when he regained consciousness was of pain. Unrelenting, agonizing pain. Every inch of his body seemed to burn with the after-effects of whatever Symeon had done to him. Evrain imagined the punishment must have continued long after he'd blacked out. His first attempt to open his eyes resulted in daggers of light stabbing into his head. He clamped his lids shut and attempted to unscramble his thoughts. Gradually his mind registered that the ache in his wrists and forearms was more severe than the burning along his thigh. Against his better judgment, he forced his eyes open again. Everything was white and for a moment he thought his sight had been damaged. He blinked a few times, eyes watering, and gradually made out a few details. The space he was in was white. All he could see was white. The walls, ceiling and floor were all the same color, almost merging together. The brightness hurt his eyes.

He concentrated on the shadows that marked out corners and gradually the room took shape. It wasn't large, just a cube roughly ten feet on each side. The surfaces had a slight sheen, reflecting the light from glowing panels set in the ceiling. Evrain attempted to feel his surroundings through his power but got nothing. He was still blocked.

He tilted his head back, which told him that Symeon's collar was still around his neck. His arms were stretched above his head, his wrists bound with plastic cable ties, which in turn were linked to a length of thick nylon rope, attached to a plastic eyelet in the ceiling. His arms were streaked with blood from where the ties had cut into his skin. The red was almost a relief amidst all the white that surrounded him. As he moved, his body twisted a little. His bare feet were only just touching the floor and all his weight was hanging from his arms. It was excruciatingly painful and he realized that he must have been hanging for some time, though there was no way of telling how long. His watch and clothes were gone, replaced by a white nylon jumpsuit of sorts. The sleeves were cut off so his arms were bare. It could have been worse. They, whoever *they* were, could have stripped him naked. They'd left him his dignity, but he did wonder how long that would last. *Someone* had taken his clothes and put him in the overalls. He didn't enjoy the idea that members of the Octis Coven may have seen him in all his glory.

You deserve this, you idiot, how could you be so fucking stupid? A range of curses flashed through Evrain's head. He'd been complacent and Symeon Malus had taken full advantage. He prayed that Dominic was still safe. Gregory was going to be furious and rightly so.

There were no windows, no door, no air vents and no plausible means of escape from his clinical prison that Evrain could detect. The air was cool but not cold so he knew that there had to be some form of temperature control. He also guessed that someone was probably watching him but that any instruments or cameras were placed well out of his view or behind concealment spells.

He jerked his arms hard, testing the robustness of the bindings around his wrists, but only succeeded in making the plastic dig even further into his flesh. He moaned as his body swung helplessly from side to side while he attempted to regain his balance on his toes. A warm trickle of fresh blood slid down one arm. It was somewhat ironic that the Coven was after his blood and here he was, donating freely.

Gregory had warned him that the Octis Coven was not to be taken lightly. Their resources were all too apparent in the prison they'd created for him. They understood that an elemental warlock would not be able to take advantage of his power without access to natural resources, collared or not. Even the air in the claustrophobic space was recycled, though Evrain suspected he might be able to manipulate it anyway. The precautions seemed extreme considering the blocking collar around his neck. Someone wanted him to suffer.

As he hung there, helpless, he tried to focus his mind on something other than the pain he was in. He had to fight down a rising sense of panic. His captivity had been planned with care and he could see no obvious way out—even if he hadn't been suspended like a fish on a hook. Octis had gone to great deal of trouble to contain him. It made sense that they must also understand that for him to channel, Dominic would have to be close by. They would need to take Dominic as well. Evrain's head ached viciously and the edges of his vision began to close in. His last thought before the darkness claimed him again was of Dominic and the danger that he must be in.

* * * *

Evrain's second journey back into the light was accompanied by the gloating sound of Symeon's voice—though the man himself was not present, his rasping tones filled the room. Evrain had the feeling Symeon had been talking for a while. He was glad he'd missed at least some of his monologue.

"How are you feeling, Evrain? Uncomfortable, I hope."

Evrain ignored the taunting and remained silent. Discomfort did not begin to describe the pain he was in. He wondered if he would ever feel his arms again. As a practitioner of bondage he was very aware of the dangers of misplaced knots and pressure against arteries and nerves. He doubted anyone would have checked when they were suspending him.

"I'm sure you would like the pain to end, though I myself would prefer that it continue as long as possible." Symeon's cackle lived up to the stereotype of every evil villain ever created. It made Evrain remember a horror movie marathon he and Dominic had enjoyed one night. Vincent Price and Peter Cushing had nothing on Symeon Malus.

"It's just a matter of time and I will have that pretty little boyfriend of yours to play with again. I made him very beautiful, didn't I? Do you think of me every time you fuck him?"

Evrain did not give Symeon the satisfaction of a reaction, though it was all he could do to maintain a blank expression. Instead he ran through all the ways it might be possible for Symeon to die — slowly and painfully.

"There's no escape for you, Evrain. Your cell has been very carefully designed. These bitches want you badly. They'll bleed you dry and I'll laugh while they do it." He paused, presumably for effect. "What, no witty come back, no sharp retort? I'm disappointed in you."

Not as much as I'm disappointed in myself.

"I've waited patiently for this. You must have known that I would take my revenge for what you and the aging excuse for a warlock, Gregory, did to me that day in Inkcap Glade. The two of you were lucky. I killed your grandmother easily enough. A whelp like you is hardly a worthy challenge."

Evrain had to hide his shock that Symeon had admitted to Agatha's murder with such nonchalance. He'd suspected it, of course, though he still didn't know how Symeon had managed it. The confirmation of his suspicions turned his blood to ice.

"You know, seeing you helpless like this will fuel my wet dreams for months to come." Symeon's conversational tone was sickening. "I'll be thinking of you when I fuck Damon's useless ass. After I've given him the whipping he deserves, of course."

Evrain moaned at the unwanted picture that invaded his mind. "Christ, Symeon, can't you just torture me in a more traditional way? Get the electrodes out or something, but don't subject to me to thoughts of you and Damon together, that's just too cruel." Evrain hoped Damon was still safe with Nathaniel.

"Fuck you, Evrain. Say what you will, this time the last word will be mine."

There was a click, then silence. Evrain heaved a sigh of relief. He would rather face the whole Octis Coven and whatever torture they had in store than listen to Symeon for a second longer. Symeon's absence did have a downside — there was nothing to distract Evrain from his aching body or his fear for Dominic. He gritted his teeth and amused himself by imagining all the things he would do to Symeon once he got free. Some of them were impossible, even using magic, but it was amusing to picture him with a tail or staked out as lunch for a nest of fire ants. Evisceration had potential, as did melting or crushing by a tornado-flung house. He was straying into Oz territory. The pain had to be affecting his mind.

In front of him a thin vertical line appeared on the wall. At first Evrain thought he was imagining things but then a panel slid sideways with a hiss. The door had been so well shielded it had been invisible — to him at least. Three women entered his prison, one standing slightly in front of the other two. The door slid closed behind them.

"Mr. Brookes, my name is Imelda Krenick. I can only offer my deepest apologies for the way you have been treated. Get him down from there immediately." She gestured and her two companions stepped forward. One gripped Evrain's hips while the other reached up to cut the plastic ties around his wrists.

Even with support, Evrain dropped heavily. The women did their best to catch him and as a result he didn't hit the floor too hard, but the fire that rushed through his arms, combined with fatigue, turned his vision red then black.

When he came around, Evrain found himself lying on a low cot. He was handcuffed but the cuffs were made of heavy plastic rather than metal. Beneath the cuffs his wrists had been lightly bandaged and the streaks of blood had been washed from his arms.

"The restraints are a precaution, but necessary to protect my colleagues." Imelda stood as if she were at attention on a military parade ground, not a single muscle relaxed. "You are a powerful young man, Mr. Brookes, and I'm afraid Symeon Malus has cast my coven in an extremely poor light—something I regret. I would not blame you for being furious."

Evrain sat up with care. He still hurt everywhere but had no desire to be sitting while Imelda loomed over him. He stood then met her cold blue eyes with an unwavering gaze of his own.

"Your friends have left? How long was I out?"

"Just a few minutes," Imelda replied. "I wanted to talk to you alone. I thought you might be more comfortable that way."

And to demonstrate your position of power. Evrain shrugged and immediately regretted the action. The abused muscles in his arms, neck and shoulders were united in their disapproval of movement. "Your apologies are meaningless while you keep me here against my will. Kidnap and imprisonment are federal crimes in this country, I believe."

"And you and I both know it is not in our interest to involve law enforcement agencies in our business."

"What do you want, Imelda? You didn't come in here for small talk and you certainly didn't go to all this effort"—he gestured with his bound hands—"to contain me, without some end game in mind. This place and enlisting Symeon's help must have cost you a fortune, so what's the payoff?"

"Perhaps it *is* better to get straight to the point, but first I'm sure you would like to freshen up. I will arrange some food, then we'll talk. Please don't attempt to resist my colleagues. You're weak. The collar you have on blocks your power. I don't want to hurt you any more than I have to but if you attempt to escape, I won't hesitate."

The same two women Evrain had seen before he'd blacked out came back into the room, leaving the door open. They both held slender batons, which Evrain eyed with suspicion.

"The advances in electroshock equipment have been quite remarkable in recent years," Imelda said. "These won't kill you but you won't enjoy the sensation, so please don't do anything to encourage their use."

Evrain sighed. He was in no condition to fight a teddy bear, let alone two armed women with a fetish for abusing warlocks. "A trip to the bathroom would be welcome," he said. "A meal even more so. I promise to behave." *For a while at least.*

The trip to the facilities revealed little. A short plastic-coated passage led to a washroom capsule made from molded acrylic, similar to the pods he'd seen in cheap European motels. There was nothing Evrain could use as a weapon. He was given some privacy to use the toilet and splash water on his face. He wondered if he could manipulate the water and attempted to reach for his power. All he got for his trouble was a stabbing pain behind his eyes and the collar around his neck warmed to an uncomfortable heat. It was an effective block. He was then escorted back to his cell. Two plastic chairs had been added to the furnishings. Imelda occupied one. On her knees was a tray holding a plastic-wrapped sandwich, a bag of chips and a polystyrene beaker of water.

"I realize that under normal circumstances you could kill me with the water," she said.

Evrain took the other seat then accepted the drink she held out to him. "Yes, I could."

"But you wouldn't because you were brought up with morals and since coming into your power you've been guided by people with strong ethical values."

"Even very patient people can be driven to extreme actions, Imelda." Evrain drank the water. He didn't think Imelda would stoop to drugging him and he was thirsty. The sandwich was fresh and hunger made him eat with undignified haste. "How long have I been here?"

"A few hours. Symeon neglected to tell me of your arrival...for some time." Imelda did not sound impressed.

"Why are you working with that worm?"

"He has his uses. Only another warlock could get that collar on you. Gregory Thanet is your godfather. Nathaniel Alberich is his ally. I was left with little option, but Malus has served his purpose. He got you here but our association is temporary, regardless of what he might think."

"You still haven't told me why I'm here."

"No, I haven't. It's very simple. I need your blood."

Evrain snorted. "So do I, Imelda."

Her parody of a smile didn't reach her eyes. "A single drop of warlock's blood can increase the potency of a potion one hundred fold. I don't want much, I'm not greedy. A few vials will suffice — certainly not more than you can spare."

"And I suppose your use of these potions is entirely altruistic?" Evrain knew better. The Coven sought influence and power. How they got it didn't matter.

Imelda shrugged. "The way I conduct my business is not your concern."

"If you just wanted blood you could have taken it when I was unconscious." Evrain checked his bare arms but there was no sign of puncture marks.

"That's because I need you to be channeling when I take it."

"You have to be kidding me?" Evrain gave a short, harsh laugh. "Never going to happen."

"And that's why I couldn't just waltz up to your front door and ask you politely." Imelda stood then brushed a microscopic piece of lint from her pants.

"You could have tried! This is not the best way to go about securing my cooperation."

"Which is why Symeon is earning his keep at this very moment. I know you need your partner to channel. Symeon will bring Dominic Castine here. Then we will talk again."

Evrain shot to his feet so fast his chair clattered to the floor. He picked it up, thinking it might make a potential weapon. Even collared he could try to escape. Before he could attack Imelda the door slid open. The two women wielding stun batons got between him and Imelda. One of them struck. Evrain lifted the chair in an attempt to protect himself but the baton made contact with his arm. The jolt knocked him to the ground where another strike hit his hip. He writhed in pain, lights flashing in front of his eyes. When his vision cleared he was alone. The three women and the chairs were gone, leaving just him and the cot in the room. Evrain managed to get to his feet. He stared at the white walls, frustration seething through his body.

"Touch him, Imelda, hurt him in any way and there will be nowhere you can hide from me." He really hoped the witch was listening.

Chapter Ten

Dominic dozed in one of the armchairs next to the fire. He wasn't fully asleep, but he was exhausted by the day's events and it helped to close his eyes and absorb the heat of the flames. Coryn had been keeping the hearth supplied with logs and a few twitches of Gregory's fingers kept it well ablaze. Warlocks were handy for some things. Shadow stretched out on the rug at Dominic's feet, snoring and twitching. A saucepan sat on the ancient stove in the kitchen, its contents bubbling away. The air was scented with apricots.

Dominic jerked from his doze when the cottage door opened, admitting Nathaniel and Coryn. Coryn had several pizza boxes stacked precariously in his arms.

"Any trouble?" Gregory asked from his seat at the kitchen table.

"We were followed back, at a distance," Nathaniel replied. "I'm sure it was Symeon. There was no sign of anyone on the path but he'll be getting into position. Do you want me to go deal with him?" Nathaniel sounded like he would relish doing just that.

"No." Gregory yawned. "He's right where we want him to be. Let's eat. We all need the fuel."

Dominic ambled across to the table, lifted one of the pizza box lids then inhaled. "Smells great. I just need to check the agrimony." He peered into the saucepan on the stove and gave it a stir. "I'd guess this needs another half an hour or so. Do you know what you're going to do with it yet?"

"I have an idea. I need to discuss it with Nathaniel." Gregory spread the pizza boxes across the table. "Tell me there's no pineapple on any of these."

"Coryn warned me." Nathaniel laughed. "Though what you have against fruit is a mystery to me." He leaned over to extract a slice of pizza. Strings of mozzarella clung tenaciously to the box.

"Pineapple is an abomination. There's a reason it's covered in that thick skin. If we were meant to eat it we'd be able to peel it. Like a banana," Gregory declared.

"Don't bother to argue with him." Coryn shook his head. "I've had the debate with him so many times I've lost count."

Nathaniel shrugged then sat down to eat. Dominic joined them at the table. Now he wasn't alone his appetite had returned. The four men munched steadily, washing the pizza down with fresh apple juice. Dominic got the feeling the conversation wouldn't get more serious until Gregory and Nathaniel could talk in private. "Want to join me by the fire, Coryn?"

Coryn rolled his eyes. "Sure. We'll let the big bad warlocks get to their plotting. I'm sure they'll let us in on the plans eventually." He blew a kiss at Gregory, who mock-glared back.

Dominic returned to his armchair. On the rug, Shadow rolled onto her back, legs in the air, exposing her ample belly. Dominic shook his head. "She already acts like she owns the place."

"Ah, but she does." Coryn joined him, taking the other chair. "You are just a puny human, slave to feline kind. Get used to it."

"I think she's a bit more than just a cat," Dominic suggested, feeling a bit stupid for voicing the thought.

"Oh, definitely. Gregory thinks she's a guardian, drawn to Evrain. There's no point in fighting it."

"She's too rotund to make a good guard-cat," Dominic said. Shadow leapt onto his lap, sinking her claws into his thighs before settling in a furry heap.

Coryn laughed. "She stopped you from going out, didn't

she?"

Dominic didn't have an answer for that. At the kitchen table, Gregory and Nathaniel sat talking, deep in discussion about the properties of agrimony from what Dominic could make out.

"Relax," Coryn chided. "They'll tell us when they have a workable plan."

"I can't relax. Not while Symeon, or Octis, has Evrain. What are they doing to him, Coryn? He could be hurt..."

"Evrain is strong. They need him in one piece, remember? I'm not going to tell you not to worry. If I were in your position I'd be feeling exactly the same. But you also have to save your strength for whatever rescue attempt Gregory and Nathaniel cook up. Evrain will need you."

"I want him back, Coryn. Every arrogant, controlling, dominant inch of him."

"I do understand. You're two halves of a whole now, just like Gregory and I. I think it's likely Nathaniel and Damon will be the same, don't you?"

Dominic nodded. "Seems probable. They already have strong feelings for each other, don't they?"

"It happens that way. The connections we have are powerful."

Dominic couldn't disagree. Even after a short time together, he couldn't imagine life without Evrain. He hoped he wouldn't have to find out what it might be like.

He and Coryn sat in companionable silence while Nathaniel and Gregory talked in low but urgent voices. Dominic itched to do something, anything. He hated sitting around while Evrain was suffering.

"Stop thinking about it," Coryn said.

"About what?"

"About what Symeon might be doing to him. It doesn't do you, or him, any good."

"I can't help it. Symeon hates Evrain's guts."

"Symeon hates everyone...apart from himself."

"I wish..." Dominic didn't finish. He didn't want to

verbalize what he was thinking. He didn't like himself very much for thinking it.

"You wish Gregory and Evrain had ended him when they had the chance?"

Dominic nodded. "And I'm ashamed for thinking it."

"Don't be. Symeon Malus has incited those feelings in all of us at one time or another. Doesn't mean we stoop to his level and act on them. You wouldn't really want Evrain to use his gift to kill, would you?"

"No." Dominic shook his head. "That would hurt him. Inside, you know?"

"I do. Hey, looks like we're being invited back to the big kids' table."

Dominic peered over his shoulder to see Gregory gesturing in their direction. "Finally! I'd better check the pan first." He relocated Shadow back to the rug amid a few loud protests before walking across to the stove. The agrimony had steeped well so he turned the burner off and put the pan to one side. Content with the potion, he joined the others at the table.

"So, do we have a plan?" He looked eagerly from Nathaniel to Gregory. They both had serious expressions and Dominic's heart fell. "You haven't worked anything out?"

"We have." Gregory steepled his fingers. "It's not ideal but it's the only thing we can think of that has a hope in hell of working. We've decided that it will be less obvious if we leave in the morning. Not first thing. I want Symeon to have plenty of opportunity to get into a position."

"It makes sense," Nathaniel added, "because he'd expect us to try to move you under cover of darkness and I want to avoid doing anything he expects. It should throw him off balance and he'll be less suspicious. He'll also have to wait out there all night."

"You'll let him take me then?" The room felt suddenly cold.

"Yes, we will." Gregory nodded. "But there's more.

Coryn, could you strain the agrimony please?"

"Sure."

Dominic watched as Coryn poured the contents through a muslin cloth into a jar. The liquid in the jar was green with a hint of gold. He carried it over, placing it on the table.

"Evrain isn't going to like this when he finds out about it." Gregory stated the obvious. He looked at Nathaniel, who stared back at him implacably. "But what he doesn't know can't hurt him."

"What exactly is it you need to do?" Dominic was beginning to feel anxious.

"Are you going to tell him or shall I?" Nathaniel asked.

"You're the empathetic one, you can tell him." Gregory smiled.

Nathaniel grimaced. "You owe me for this, Gregory."

Dominic hunched forward in his chair, fingers knitted together. "You both look so serious, what is it? One of you has to tell me or we'll be here all night."

"We think we've worked out a way to get the taint into Evrain's blood," Nathaniel said.

"Then why do you look as if you are going to tell me the world is ending? Finding a way to do this is good, isn't it?" Dominic chewed on his lower lip and waited for Nathaniel to tell him the worst. The warlock pressed his knuckles against his own temples, kneading in circles. He took a deep breath before meeting Dominic's gaze.

"Gregory will distill your brew to increase its potency, then paint it onto your skin. He will design it in such a way that it will be invisible to everyone but me, Nathaniel, you and Evrain. To him, it will seem like a set of tattoos, glowing with a magical signature—a message if you like, telling him what to do, in case you are not able to tell him yourself. He will need to absorb the potion by physical contact, so Gregory intends to put it in every place that Evrain might touch to increase our chances."

"That doesn't sound so bad," Dominic said. "What's the catch? There must be one for the pair of you to be so worried."

"When the liquid adheres to your skin, it's going to hurt. A lot." Nathaniel sighed. "I can't really explain it, but the spell will literally burn the liquid into your flesh—at least that's what it will feel like. Tattoos inked with acid. There is always a price to pay for this kind of magic, Dominic. Unfortunately in this case the person paying will be you."

Dominic swallowed. He suspected his skin might be a couple of shades lighter. "You said Gregory would put this stuff everywhere Evrain might touch. Everywhere?"

Nathaniel nodded sympathetically as Dominic's tired mind processed what that might mean. "If there's any other way, we can't think of it." Nathaniel ducked his head. "We need to do it now, to give you some recovery time before we leave in the morning."

Dominic just nodded, not trusting himself to speak.

Gregory came and stood behind Dominic's chair, resting his hands on his trembling shoulders. "Evrain would *not* want us to do this, Dominic. He would never let me hurt you, however good my intentions."

"Then it's a good thing he has no say, isn't it?" Dominic stood, pushing shaky fingers through his hair. "What do you need me to do?"

"Coryn will take you upstairs and help you get ready. I'll be with you shortly."

Dominic felt like a condemned prisoner heading for his execution as he climbed the stairs with Coryn close behind him. Nathaniel and Gregory hadn't tried to hide anything. What he was about to do was going to hurt. He suspected it wasn't going to be the good kind of pain either. He was scared but it didn't matter. This was something he had to do for Evrain.

Upstairs, Coryn squeezed his hands. "I'll leave you to take a shower. Make sure you rinse all the soap from your skin. This isn't about smelling good, it's about having a clean surface for the agrimony ink. I would be asking you to shave all the hair from your body, but that's not necessary, is it?"

Dominic gave a wry smile. "Thanks to Symeon, no it's not."

The bathroom proved to be something of a sanctuary. Dominic tried not to think about anything. He had a trick he'd been taught as a child when he would try to sleep after a nightmare—to imagine a blank wall. It had always worked better for him than counting sheep but he did have a tendency to picture varieties of moss and lichens between the bricks. On this occasion, it wasn't working and the shower didn't take nearly long enough. He rinsed carefully then toweled off. Evrain's bathrobe was on the back of the door so he put it on in the hope it might feel like Evrain was hugging him. It wasn't anywhere near as good as the real thing but Evrain's scent helped a bit. He took a few deep breaths then went to join Coryn in the bedroom.

Coryn's eyes were full of sympathy. "Gregory won't be long."

"I'm in no rush," Dominic said. "No pressing social engagements in my diary tonight."

"You'll need to take the robe off, then lie down on the bed." Coryn patted the covers. "I also have to tie you down so you don't thrash around while Gregory's working on you."

Dominic's face heated. He was sure he must be the shade of a ripe tomato. Only Evrain ever saw him naked.

Coryn chuckled. "There's no need to be shy, boy. Close your eyes if it makes you feel more comfortable."

Dominic loosed the robe's belt then shrugged the garment from his shoulders. He climbed onto the bed. "You want me on my back or front first?"

"On your back, please, and I know this is a really stupid thing to say, but try to relax."

"There's rope in the closet," Dominic offered. Evrain's bondage ropes would be kinder against his skin than anything Gregory might find in the kitchen.

"I'd never have guessed."

Coryn's wry tone made Dominic laugh. "You too, huh?"

"That would be telling." Coryn found the short lengths of soft rope then used two of them to bind Dominic's ankles to the bed's corner posts. "Arms out to your sides, I think, rather than above your head."

Dominic stretched out his arms. He kept still while Coryn tied him in place. In his head he just kept repeating *I'm doing this for Evrain, I'm doing this for Evrain.*

"Sorry, Dominic. I think I'm going to have to prop you up a bit." Coryn shoved a pillow beneath the small of Dominic's back. "Much better. I can see more skin now."

"Oh God." Dominic squeezed his eyes shut with embarrassment. Evrain loved to tie him up and usually the feeling of helplessness was a huge turn-on for him. Being manhandled by an elderly friend did not compare, though Coryn was being as gentle and considerate as he could be under the circumstances. "This had better work."

"It will. It has to."

Dominic opened his eyes. The lines around Coryn's eyes had deepened with worry. He patted Dominic's shoulder.

"You're a very brave young man. Evrain would be proud of you. He will be, when he finds out about all this." Coryn took a step back. "You'll do. I'll go and see where Gregory has gotten to."

No sooner had Coryn turned toward the door than Gregory appeared. He was holding a small, stoppered vial of a deep green liquid.

"I was just coming to find you," Coryn said. "Dominic is prepared."

"I can see that." Gregory gave Dominic a wink that made him wish there was a pillow over his face. "You'll need to gag him, though. We can't have him screaming and alerting anyone outside that something's going on. I can't use my power to silence him because it might affect what I need to do with the agrimony."

"Would they be able to hear through the wards?" Dominic asked.

"It's possible," Gregory mused. "Their senses may be enhanced for just that reason."

Coryn gave Dominic a questioning glance. Dominic sighed. His humiliation was complete. "There's a wooden chest in the bottom of the closet, there will be something you can use in there."

After a bit of rummaging Coryn returned with a thick rubber bit gag. "This is big enough that you won't be able to make much noise around it and it might help if you have something to bite down on."

Dominic opened his mouth and let Coryn insert the bit. He lifted his head so Coryn could fasten the strap.

"There. Not too tight?"

Dominic shook his head.

"I can leave if you'd prefer," Coryn said. Dominic shook his head again. He wanted Coryn to be there. He wiggled his fingers and Coryn got the message. He settled on the side of the bed and took Dominic's hand.

Gregory stood at the end of the bed. He didn't meet Dominic's eyes. "I'll be as quick as I can, Dominic. I'm going to paint this stuff over most of your body. You may be able to persuade Imelda that in order to convince Evrain to cooperate, you need to be alone with him for a while. If it works, encourage him to make love to you. If it doesn't, any contact between you will help."

Dominic felt like he was dreaming as Gregory began to mutter incomprehensible words and make intricate gestures with his fingers over the length of his body. When Gregory removed the stopper from the bottle, an emerald mist rose from its neck. Involuntarily, Dominic tensed. Coryn began to stroke his hair, offering comfort as the glittering cloud swirled, divided and came together again. Misty tendrils began to dance in the air, winding and twisting, faster and faster. Then Gregory stopped talking. His hands stilled and ribbons of vapor descended to lay themselves on Dominic's flesh. The first touch was agonizing, the burn of intense cold, then fire. Needles of pain stabbed into his skin over and over again. Dominic spasmed against his bonds, limbs straining. The gag muffled his screams as the pain went on and on.

Beads of sweat formed on Gregory's forehead as he watched intricate patterns of silver-green appear, first on the side of Dominic's neck below his ear, then across his chest, spreading out from each dark nipple. The patterns started materializing lower, delicate lines winding toward his groin. As the etching reached the base of his cock and began to spiral along its length, Dominic moaned pitifully. Tears streamed down his face and his head jerked from side to side. Fine lines of pale green, drawn by an invisible hand, patterned his hips and thighs.

Gregory checked the vial of liquid. It was still half full. He replaced the stopper then gave it a shake.

"We need to turn him over." It was difficult to keep the tension from his voice. There was no accusation in Coryn's eyes. He nodded.

"I'll untie him." Coryn circled the bed, loosening then releasing Dominic's bonds. "Help me roll him. Dominic, sweetheart, we need to turn you over now, okay?"

Dominic moaned but didn't resist as he was maneuvered onto his belly. The pillow was now beneath his hips, keeping his ass in the air.

"Spread his legs as wide as possible," Gregory said.

Coryn pressed his lips together in a tight line but did as he was asked. Soon, Dominic was bound in place once more. Gregory began the process over again. Curls of color patterned the length of Dominic's spine then intensified over the swell of his ass. When the first lines traced his balls Dominic jerked then went still.

"He's blacked out," Gregory observed. He looked at Coryn across Dominic's prone body. He smiled his relief. "Thank goodness. I never thought he'd last that long. The pain must have been excruciating."

"He's very strong." Coryn undid the gag then checked

Dominic's breathing was unimpeded.

Gregory watched as the last slivers of green slipped inside Dominic's channel. He was very glad Dominic hadn't been awake to experience that part of the process. Delicate patterns now covered a significant percentage of his body. The silvery green lines seemed to sit just below the surface of his skin, catching the light when he moved.

"You can untie him now. The painful part of the process is over." Gregory rolled his shoulders, releasing some of the tension he hadn't realized had built there.

Coryn walked around the bed, untying the restraints. "His wrists and ankles have been rubbed raw despite the soft bonds."

"We'll let him sleep now. He's going to hurt everywhere when he wakes up, so let's give him some respite while we can. I'm sure there will be some salve downstairs that you can use on those rope burns." Gregory pulled a quilt over Dominic's sleeping form, the lines of pain now smoothed from his face. "He really is beautiful, isn't he?"

Coryn nodded. He pushed a strand of dark copper hair away from Dominic's closed eyes. "Beautiful and brave. Evrain is lucky to have him."

"Just as I'm lucky to have you. They remind me of us a few years ago." Gregory took his partner's hand and gave it a squeeze.

"Only a few?" Coryn chuckled. "And neither of us was ever that good looking. I fell for your charm, obviously."

"Still a brat even after all these years."

"And you wouldn't have me any other way." Coryn pulled Gregory from the room. "Salve. Come on. Then we'll take turns sitting with him."

* * * *

Dominic tossed and turned in sleep colored by vivid nightmares where patterned snakes crawled over his body, sinking their fangs in where they pleased. Every now and again he was aware of a cool cloth resting against his burning forehead and the press of a glass against his lips. When he finally regained full consciousness, Coryn's smiling face was the first thing he saw. The silver in Coryn's hair glittered, giving him a halo of light.

"It's sunny. What time is it?" Dominic got the words out despite his dry tongue.

"Around nine," Coryn responded. "How do you feel?" He offered a glass of water so Dominic heaved himself into a sitting position.

"Like I've been chewed on by a bad tempered gator then spat out in small pieces." He took a long drink before handing the glass back. "Thanks." He lifted the quilt to look down at himself. "Holy crap!" He prodded his thigh experimentally. "Well, at least it doesn't hurt anymore."

"Just think about the upside of this," Coryn said.

"There's an upside to being covered in magical doodles?" He raised his eyebrows in question.

"Evrain is going to have to touch every bit of you in order to absorb the potion."

Dominic's cock jerked. Heat flooded his body and he knew he must be blushing from knees to neck. He yanked the quilt a bit further up his body, ignoring Coryn's laughter.

"You need to get yourself ready to leave then come down for some breakfast. Gregory is charcoaling some toast, I believe. No showering for obvious reasons."

"Okay, I'll see you downstairs."

"Oh—and you might want to consider other preparations..." Coryn suggested.

"What do you...? Oh." Realization dawned and Dominic's skin heated even further.

"You passed out before the potion worked its way inside you. As Gregory mentioned yesterday evening, at some point it would be useful if you can persuade Evrain to make love to you. The transfer of the agrimony will work much quicker that way. I doubt you'll have easy access to lube."

"How the hell did I get myself into this?" Dominic

muttered. "I understand, Coryn."

Coryn's expression was a cross between apologetic and amused. "Gregory wants to be away around mid-morning. He has another plan to make your capture seem more realistic."

"I can't wait to hear it," Dominic mumbled but found he was talking to a closed door.

* * * *

Coryn wasn't kidding about the quality of Gregory's cooking. Dominic ended up tossing his efforts in the trash then constructing poached eggs on toast for all of them. Shadow wound around his ankles, purring. Nathaniel made coffee as his contribution, not hiding his interest in the patterns over Dominic's skin.

"You can look, Nathaniel. I know you want to," Dominic offered.

"An offer I can't possibly refuse." Nathaniel traced his fingers along Dominic's arms. He examined his neck then lifted his shirt. "They've taken incredibly well, Gregory. You did good work here."

"Dominic did the hard part."

"It wasn't fun," Dominic admitted. "I hope it's something I never have to go through again." He slipped around Nathaniel to take his seat at the table. "I have an appetite, that's for sure." His stomach rumbled in agreement.

After they'd eaten and Shadow had consumed a sizeable dish of canned sardines, Dominic gave Gregory an enquiring glance. "So, what's the plan?"

"Coryn and Nathaniel are going to leave first. I want Symeon to think we are trying to trick him into believing you're leaving. Nathaniel will borrow some of your clothes. It's fortunate you have similar builds and not too much of a height difference. Do you have a hooded top, because your hair is a complete giveaway?"

"Sure, but Symeon's not going to fall for it."

"I don't want him to. I want him to think he's being clever by not following Nathaniel and Coryn. We'll wait a half hour or so, then leave. We'll act as if we assume he's gone after the others. You pretend to have forgotten something. I'll continue on to the car. That's when he'll take you—if he's going to."

"He will," Nathaniel said. "Symeon's arrogance is one of his many weaknesses. He'll believe he's outsmarted us and he won't be able to resist taking his chance. He has too much riding on delivering Dominic to Octis not to."

Fifteen minutes later, wearing their makeshift disguises, Nathaniel and Coryn stepped into the sunshine. It was just before mid-morning. They hurried down the path, trailed by Shadow, and Dominic soon lost sight of them.

"I hope they'll be okay."

"Nathaniel will keep a close eye on Coryn, don't worry. I wouldn't send him out there if I didn't know Nathaniel could wipe Symeon off the face of the planet without even breaking a sweat."

"So why hasn't he?" The question came out before Dominic could stop it.

"Because he, like me, is not a cold blooded killer."

"Sorry. I should connect my brain before I open my mouth."

"It's a natural question. If I, or Nathaniel, had dealt with Symeon years ago then you and Evrain would have been saved a great deal of trouble. We've come close a few times, I can tell you, but I've never used my power to kill, and I hope I never will. I imagine Nathaniel feels the same. That's the difference between us and Symeon. He has the ethics of a rattlesnake on crack."

Dominic nodded. "I get it. What do you think is up with the fur-ball? That's the first time since she arrived that she's shown any interest in going out."

"Call of nature?"

"I don't believe that any more than you do," Dominic said. "You know something about that animal. Evrain did too. She's not what she seems."

"Talking of... She's back." Gregory opened the door just enough to let Shadow back inside. She immediately jumped into his arms, uttering a series of meows.

"So what does she have to say for herself?" Dominic asked, half joking.

"It's warm. The mice are sleeping. Symeon is still in the woods waiting and there's someone with him." Gregory was absolutely serious.

Dominic had no reply. Shadow turned her green gaze on him and he could have sworn she was smiling. He had no time to debate the merits of a supernatural pet because a few minutes later he and Gregory slipped down the path from Hornbeam Cottage, then into the lane. They moved quickly, keeping to the edge of the path, using the shadows of the trees to conceal themselves as much as possible. About halfway to the main road Dominic stopped, patting his pockets. He tapped Gregory's shoulder then whispered urgently in his ear for a few seconds. After some gesturing and frustrated signing from the older man Dominic turned and jogged back toward the cottage. He'd lost sight of Gregory around a bend in the path when a branch seemed to dip in the breeze to snag in his hair. As he pulled away, the cord holding his protective amulet worked free and dropped the ground, nestling amongst the soggy leaves.

Dominic kept going as if he hadn't noticed, though he was acutely aware of what was happening and how defenseless he now was. He listened hard but he didn't hear anyone approaching. He reached the cottage gate wondering if all Gregory's plotting and the pain he'd been through had been for nothing. It was only when he had one hand on the gate that he noticed the sudden silence. There was no birdsong and even the trees seemed to have stilled. The snap of a twig was disproportionately loud. He whirled around to get the briefest glimpse of Symeon's evil smile. He tried to scream, but a gloved hand closed around his mouth, crushing his lips. He tasted the iron of his blood as he bit his tongue.

Someone, or something, grabbed hold of his arms, the grip like steel bands around his biceps. A dark hood was pulled over his head, cutting off his sight and stifling his breath. He fought hard, pulling away only to be captured again and pushed against the gate. He tried to wrench his arms free then collapsed to his knees, becoming a dead weight. It did no good. He was dragged along the ground, stones digging into his back and shoulders. A pinpoint of pain pierced his thigh and within seconds the taste of blood and fear was replaced by comforting weightlessness.

Chapter Eleven

The low hum of an engine was the first sound to penetrate the fog muddling Dominic's thoughts. He battled the confusion, trying to work out where he was and why he couldn't see. It all came back in a rush. Being captured. The hood. He jerked but his body was restrained not just by a seatbelt but by something else. He guessed some kind of strap had been fastened around his chest and the seat, pinning his arms to his sides. It was effective. He could move his head and his legs but not much in between. He forced his rigid muscles to relax. It was pointless struggling when he wanted to be taken to wherever Evrain was being held.

"He's awake."

The voice came from behind him. There was someone in the back seat and Dominic knew who it was. He banged his head back against the seat rest in frustration. "You son of a bitch."

"Keep your mouth shut." This time it was Symeon's oily tones he heard. "Then I won't have to hurt you. For now."

Dominic clenched his fingers into fists, wishing he could use them to inflict some damage.

"We will reach our destination shortly. You *will* behave… that is if you want to see your lover again." Symeon said the word lover as if he had a nasty taste in his mouth. Dominic imagined he had absolutely no understanding of love unless it was of the narcissistic kind. Symeon probably masturbated to his reflection.

Gravity pressed Dominic against his seatbelt, telling him the vehicle was heading downhill. It was moving slowly so he guessed they were heading into an underground parking garage. The grating clank of metal shutter rolling up confirmed it. He didn't know how long the drug he'd been given had kept him unconscious but several clues told him it hadn't been long. He wasn't hungry or thirsty and his bladder wasn't screaming at him. The vehicle stopped. A metallic grinding signaled the rise of a door before it moved forward again. This time when it stopped, the engine was silenced. Rustling and the heavy clunk of car doors told Dominic that Symeon and his companion had left the vehicle. There was a blast of cool air when the door next to him opened. He tried not to cringe as his seatbelt was unfastened and the strap around his body released. He was manhandled from the car, held upright by someone as his knees buckled. It was hard to balance without his sight.

"Don't try to run," Symeon said. "A bullet in the leg tends to offend."

Dominic didn't doubt Symeon would use a gun and probably enjoy it. He stayed pliant, allowing himself to be tugged along. He listened, detecting the slide of elevator doors then the stab of a button being pressed. The elevator rose smoothly. It had to be a large building because the ascent took a while. When the doors opened again he was guided out and this time there was plush carpet beneath his feet rather than concrete. He counted thirty paces in a straight line before he was jerked to a halt. There was a click before he was pushed into another area. A kick buckled his knees and he dropped into a chair.

He found he was breathing fast and attempted to draw in air more slowly. The bag was yanked from his head. He blinked as his eyes burned in the bright light. He assessed his surroundings. He was seated in a leather office chair in front of a console desk upon which sat a state-of-the-art monitor, keyboard and hard drive. The room was small and there was no other furniture. Symeon stood next to him and he was alone. Dominic found it difficult to meet Symeon's eyes. They glinted red and seemed to contain pure hatred.

"I want you to take a look at some footage I filmed earlier. I think you'll enjoy it." Symeon's smile chilled Dominic's blood. Facing the monitor was an improvement on having to look at him, but it displayed images that Dominic didn't want to accept. Evrain hung helplessly in the center of a pure white room. His eyes flickered open and closed, his face deathly pale and drawn. Streaks of blood ran from beneath the bindings around his wrists. Cuts and grazes decorated his bare arms.

"Let him go, Symeon! You can't do this."

Symeon just gave him a malevolent glare before zooming the picture in. "He deserves every second of the pain he's experiencing."

Dominic half stood. Symeon shoved him back into the chair.

"Behave. Your time will come but I need something from Evrain first. Then you and I will be spending some quality time together."

Bile rose in Dominic's throat. "He's not going to give you anything. Symeon, you're deranged." Dominic whispered the words almost to himself.

"Oh, I'm sure that now *you* have joined us Evrain will be a little more compliant. He'll give me what I want, thinking he can save you. He can't, of course. I can't wait to tie you down and fuck you until you scream."

"What happened to make you so evil, Symeon?"

Symeon brushed a hand through his long white hair, blinked once then hit Dominic hard across the face. "When I start torturing you in front of him I'm sure Evrain will be only too willing to give me anything I ask for."

"That is not going to happen, Symeon. We are not animals, unlike you, it seems."

Dominic hadn't heard the door open. He twisted around to see who had spoken. The woman who stood in the doorway was so nondescript in appearance that she could have faded into any crowd, but she radiated authority and power. At her shoulder, two other women hovered attentively.

"Dominic Castine, I presume? My name is Imelda Krenick. Mr. Malus works for me. A situation that will continue no longer. I must apologize as he seems to have, yet again, overstepped his bounds." She moved forward and stared at the monitor. "What you're seeing happened a while ago. I put a stop to it. Mr. Malus was told to contain Mr. Brookes, not torture him. This is the live feed." She pressed a couple of keys and the image in front of Dominic changed.

"He's too dangerous to pamper, Imelda," Symeon whined.

"You are dismissed, Symeon. I don't want to see you again. Do you understand me?"

"We have an agreement." Symeon seemed to shrink in stature beneath Imelda's withering glare.

"One I have more than fulfilled. You, however, have flouted my orders and abused my trust. Our relationship is over."

If Symeon had possessed a tail, it would have been tucked between his legs as he slunk out of the room, casting one last threatening look in Dominic's direction. Dominic ignored him, turning back to stare at the screen, which now showed Evrain lying on a low cot in his white cell. His hands were cuffed but he appeared to be sleeping.

"Now. Perhaps you and I can have a sensible conversation, Dominic. I may call you Dominic?"

Dominic swiveled his chair around to face her. He gave a brief nod. It was a concession he could afford.

"I know you want to go to him, but we need to have a little chat first."

She turned to her colleagues. "The two of you may leave. I'm not in any danger from Mr. Castine."

Dominic didn't know whether to feel insulted or threatened. Imelda leaned against the frame of the still open door. Her smile didn't reach her eyes and Dominic knew he was facing someone just as ruthless as Symeon, albeit rather more civilized.

"I'll get straight to the point, Dominic. My requirements are very simple. All I want is a vial or two of Evrain's blood, given while he channels. Once I have my supply then you will both be free to go." She pursed her red-glossed lips. "I know he has some old-fashioned values when it comes to use of his power and that is why you are here. I'm going to give you one hour to convince him to cooperate with me. I'm sure you can be very persuasive. I hope you can be, because if you don't succeed then I will be forced to bring Symeon back to do things his way and I can assure you that his methods are far less pleasant than mine."

The quiet certainty in Imelda's voice was terrifying and Dominic had no doubt that she meant every word. "I have no power to force Evrain to do anything he doesn't want to," Dominic said.

"I think you do. Just make it clear to him how much you will be made to suffer if he does not comply."

Dominic bowed his head. He didn't want to give in to Imelda too easily in case she suspected his motives. "You can't keep us here forever, Imelda. People will come for us."

"No doubt. But do you want to live the rest of your life in fear, suspicious of everyone? Be assured I will keep coming after you until I get what I want."

"And what's to stop you doing this again when you run out of blood?"

"A good question." She pursed her lips. "A single drop of warlock's blood is enough to boost several potions. It is not compatible with all of them. A few vials will last decades, by which time Evrain will have aged past his usefulness. Assuming he survives at all, that is."

"Why should I trust what you're saying?"

"Because you have little choice." Imelda smiled.

Sighing, Dominic paused before he spoke. "I want some time alone with him."

Imelda frowned.

"Imelda, much as I hate this, you have a point. If you're not after Evrain then it will be someone else. I want a semblance of peace in our lives but Evrain is going to take some convincing. It's time you put a bit of trust in me, don't you think?"

"Very well. I will give you the time with him. You have my word that you will not be observed." Saying this, she turned off the monitor. "In the drawer next to you you'll find some overalls. I'm afraid I must insist you leave all your clothes here. The collar he wears blocks his power, but I have still been very careful to ensure Evrain has little access to the elements and even natural fibers are of the earth."

With a mental sigh of relief, Dominic slid the drawer open. He removed a roll of white nylon fabric. He shook it out. The one-piece garment seemed to be identical to the one Evrain wore.

He stood. Imelda didn't budge. It was clear she had no intention of leaving while he changed. He hoped that Gregory's assurance that only a select few people could see the patterns on Dominic's skin held true. He stripped off his shirt first then toed off his shoes. Socks and pants came next. He hesitated, standing in his underwear while Imelda stared at him, unblinking. He sighed, then rolled down his shorts. Dignity seemed to be a thing of the past for him. He stepped into the overalls, pulling them up with a jerk. He wriggled into the arm holes then closed the zipper with some relief.

"Thank you." A brief smile crossed Imelda's lips, making Dominic wonder exactly what she was thanking him for. "Do what you must to convince him, Dominic. I really don't want Symeon to hurt you."

"His hands…"

"Stay bound. Symeon is right to say that Evrain is dangerous. I'm giving you some latitude but I cannot free him completely."

Barefoot, Dominic trailed Imelda from the small office to the elevator where she pressed the button for the sub-basement level. Their destination had to be on the same floor as the parking garage. From the elevator it was just a short walk down a dim corridor to a single door, which opened into a vestibule of sorts.

"The door to the passage will be locked behind you," Imelda said. She gestured to the door in front of them. "This leads to Evrain's cell. The other to a small bathroom. Feel free to use the facilities if you need to. I will leave the cell door unlocked." She typed a code into the key pad next to the door. It slid open with barely a hiss then Dominic stepped inside.

The room in which Evrain was held was so white it was painful to look at. There was no relief for the eyes and, when the door closed behind Dominic, it became quite disorienting. He imagined it was akin to snow-blindness, not that he'd ever been skiing. He walked across to the cot, knelt beside Evrain's prone form then touched his bare arm.

"Evrain, it's me. Please wake up."

He was rewarded with a snarl. "I'm not asleep, just pretending in case you were Symeon." He rolled on to his back and sighed. "What in the fires of hell are you doing here, Dominic? You should be safe at home behind layers of protective wards."

"I'll explain everything, but what about you, did they hurt you very much?"

Evrain sat up awkwardly. He patted the cot. "Come sit here with me."

Dominic took a spot next to him, pressing close, thigh to thigh.

"I think my arms are a couple of inches longer, but other than that not really. Symeon roughed me up a little. The worst thing was having to listen to him gloat—that was painful on the ears."

"He showed me pictures of you hanging from the ceiling."

"Great. He'll probably have full-sized prints made for his bedroom wall."

"There's a camera in this room somewhere." Dominic examined the blank walls. "I can't see it though. Imelda promised me she wouldn't watch us."

"She will." Evrain rested his cuffed hands on his knees.

"Why are your wrists bandaged?" Dominic asked, touching Evrain's hand.

"Symeon used cable ties when he hung me up. They cut into my skin. Imelda didn't appreciate what he'd done. I don't think she sanctioned Symeon's violence."

"I got the same impression. She reamed him good after he threatened me. They aren't the best of buddies."

"I can't believe I walked into such an obvious trap," Evrain said. "I feel like a complete idiot."

"You were an idiot because you think more about my safety than your own." Dominic ran a comforting hand through Evrain's hair. He stared into his green-gold eyes. "It was only a matter of time, Evrain — the Coven would never have given up. That's why I'm here." He rested his head on Evrain's shoulder. With his mouth close to Evrain's ear, Dominic whispered the details of Gregory's plan. Then he unzipped his overalls, exposing the strange designs across his chest.

Evrain stared, his eyes wide. He raised his hands but didn't quite touch. "How do they look to you?" he asked.

"Like silvery green tattoos just beneath my skin," Dominic replied. "Gregory told me that apart from him and Nathaniel, only you and I would be able to see them. Imelda didn't notice anything and she watched while I changed into this stupid suit."

"She saw you naked?" Evrain's eyes narrowed.

Dominic shook his head. "I think we have bigger issues to worry about, don't you?"

"I suppose so. The designs seem like holograms to me. They sort of hover over your skin. When Gregory put these on you, did it hurt?"

"That doesn't matter." Dominic brushed off the question. "What's important is that we get the agrimony transferred to you. We only have an hour together before Imelda comes back."

"I'm so fucking angry that Gregory did this to you, but it just might work." Evrain scrubbed a hand through his hair, making it stand up. "Let's hope that Imelda was telling the truth when she promised not to watch. I don't get off on exhibitionism." He pulled the thin mattress from the cot then laid it on the floor. "Not much, but it will have to do."

Pulling the mattress toward the other wall, Dominic grinned. "The footage I saw had the camera pointing directly at the cot. If we put this over here we might get a bit more privacy."

Evrain sat on the mattress, his back against the wall. He crooked a finger and beckoned Dominic, a salacious look in his eyes. Dominic shrugged the overalls from his shoulders, unzipping them to the waist. He knelt across Evrain's legs and Evrain looped his arms over Dominic's head to rest on his shoulders. For a moment they just gazed into each other's eyes. Against all the odds Dominic began to get aroused. Evrain licked his lips.

"I missed you, you know. Thinking about you kept me going."

"Kiss me?" Dominic tilted his head to the side, silently encouraging Evrain to kiss his neck. Evrain obliged, running his tongue across the green patterns. A faint mist rose from Dominic's skin and slipped into Evrain's mouth. As he kissed and licked Dominic sensed the patterns dissipating, leaving pristine skin behind. There was just a faint tingle when the marks disappeared, but as Evrain worked his way toward his aching nipples, the sensation spread all over his body.

"How far down do the markings go?" Evrain whispered.

"Thighs. Back and front."

"Lose the suit."

"Back to your usual demanding self," Dominic muttered. He ducked from the circle of Evrain's arms in order to stand. He lowered the suit's zip further before wiggling until it dropped to his ankles.

"Good." Evrain unzipped his shapeless garment. "I can't

get this thing off because of the cuffs. Unzipped will have to be enough. Come here."

Dominic hugged him. Skin met skin from chest to groin — as far down as Evrain's zipper went.

"You're so warm." Evrain pushed him back a little. He sucked on one nipple then the other. Dominic moaned, throwing back his head. Green mist seemed to envelop Evrain's body.

"It's working."

"I know. I can feel it. There's a lot of power in Gregory's work." Evrain ran his hands down Dominic's body until he could cup his balls. "Lean against the wall."

They changed positions. Evrain dropped to his knees. "I can't believe Gregory decorated your cock. He and I are going to have words."

"That's not all he did, love." Dominic gasped as the moist warmth of Evrain's mouth surrounded him. His knees began to buckle as Evrain sucked his balls and cock in turn, teasing with soft skims of his tongue. Dominic's thoughts scattered. He could have been surrounded by the whole coven and he wouldn't have cared. He didn't want Evrain to stop for anything. When Evrain nipped a little harder, Dominic had to fight back a scream. It was impossible to stay completely silent while Evrain drove him to the edge of release over and over again. His back arched and he moaned, all worries about their predicament swept away by the intensity of the moment. He came without warning, spurting his release deep into Evrain's throat, shuddering with reaction. Every muscle quivered and his ass ached to be filled.

"I've got you, sweetheart." Evrain licked him clean before pulling away. He was breathing heavily, a sheen of perspiration coating his skin. "You okay?"

"Shouldn't I be asking you that?" Dominic asked. "Does it hurt you — absorbing the magic?"

"Not at all. Feels good, actually."

"Want you in me. Don't care if they're watching."

"You secretly an exhibitionist, love? Could be fun." Evrain got to his feet. "There are a few clubs I know…"

"So not the conversation for right now," Dominic complained. "My ass needs you. Now."

"So demanding. I like it. Turn around." Evrain's voice was gruff, his words abrupt with need. He pressed the length of his body against Dominic's back.

Dominic felt even teeth biting gently into his neck, then Evrain's voice sounded in his ear. "I've absorbed the potion, we don't have to do this."

"Not all of it." Dominic pushed back against him urgently. "I need you."

"He put it inside you?"

"Yes!" Dominic spat out the word as a hard cock dug into his ass.

"Fuck! There's no butter on hand this time, Dominic, it's going to hurt."

"I prepped earlier today. It will have to be enough. You have to do this, it will help you absorb the agrimony faster."

To Dominic's relief, Evrain didn't waste time with further debate. He pushed forward hard and fast, his bound hands pressing into the small of Dominic's back.

"I love you."

"Love you too." Dominic accepted the momentary burn of penetration. He clamped his lips together, not wanting to give Evrain any reason to stop. A thrill of renewed desire shot through his body as Evrain pistoned his hips back and forth.

"We can stop now…" Evrain slowed a little. "I must have absorbed everything by now."

"Don't you fucking dare, you bastard! I'm so close…" The magic had to be working on his libido, Dominic decided. There was no way he should be ready to orgasm again so soon.

"Oh…you like a little pain, do you?" Evrain punctuated his words with a thrust that shoved Dominic into the wall.

"You know I do." Dominic tried to keep quiet but it was

difficult to stay silent with Evrain thrusting into him so forcefully. Sensation was building throughout his body. He gritted his teeth and tried to contain the shout that wanted to escape his lips. He dug his nails into the palms of his hands and suppressed his cry as Evrain came with a hot gush inside him. Dominic grabbed his own cock with one hand and a couple of swift tugs brought him over the edge as well. Exhausted, he slid to the floor. Evrain collapsed next to him and they sat side by side against the wall, breathing heavily.

"Well, if anyone was watching, I think we just gave them a pretty good show." Evrain laughed and leaned across to kiss Dominic's lips.

"I'm supposed to be convincing you to give up your blood to Octis," Dominic said. "They know how stubborn you are so when Imelda gets here you're going to have to make it seem as if I haven't made a good enough argument and resist a little longer."

"If I do that," answered Evrain, "they might hurt you and that's not something I'm going to allow."

"You still need to take it to the edge and make it convincing. As it is, I'm sure they're going to suspect that something's up. Imelda doesn't seem stupid and she knows that giving her anything without resisting would go against your nature."

"Fine, I'll put on a good show, but if it gets to the point where it looks as though you're at risk, I stop straight away. Did Gregory say how long it would take for the potion to affect my blood?"

Dominic made a grab for his nylon suit. "If you absorbed everything that he put on my skin then the effect should have been instant and your blood is already useless to them. Perhaps now they'll leave you alone?" Dominic pulled the suit up, lifting his ass so he could get it over his hips. "I really need to clean up. Imelda said she'd leave the doors unlocked so we could use the bathroom." He stood, leaving his suit unzipped part way and hanging around his waist.

"I don't know how to open the door. They've used some kind of concealing spell."

Dominic wandered across to the wall where he knew the door to be. It slid open in front of him. "See, I can do magic too." He grinned.

After a quick trip to the washroom they returned to Evrain's cell. They sat on the mattress and Evrain pulled Dominic against him.

"Do you really think they're just going to let us go once they know that they've been tricked? We need to find a way to get my hands free and this fucking collar off my neck. Then we have to get out of this part of the building so that I can use my power. In here there's nothing elemental I can use."

"What about the water in the washroom?"

"The taps only deliver measured amounts of water. Not enough to do any damage with. It's useless anyway while I'm blocked."

"Well, they're going to need you to channel when they take your blood. They'll have to remove the collar then. I can't imagine they'll want you channeling in here, so we will just have to take our chance that there will be an opportunity to escape when they move us. I was drugged during the car journey down here and there was a hood over my head but I'd guess we're somewhere in downtown Portland." He paused. "There's something else. Symeon had help when he took me. There was someone else in the car on the way here. He only spoke once but I recognized the voice. I'm sure it was Damon."

"What the fuck!" Evrain's already pale skin turned a lighter shade. "That ungrateful, traitorous...he had me completely fooled."

"Look, I've no idea how much time has passed since Imelda left me with you but it must be coming up for an hour. We can worry about Damon's part in this later. We have more to fear from Symeon, especially if Imelda follows through with her threat to cut him off from the potions she's been providing. That's where the danger will come from. He'll be seeking vengeance against us *and* the Octis Coven."

"I think you're right. Finish dressing. I don't want anyone else to see you without your clothes on."

Dominic wriggled into the top part of his overalls then zipped up. He examined Evrain's wrists and winced at the fresh blood seeping from beneath the bandages under the cuffs. "I wish I had something to cut these off with."

Evrain gave him a small smile. "Take advantage while you can, my love. This is the last time I will be the one in this position, I can assure you."

Dominic rolled his eyes in exasperation and was about to make a sarcastic retort when the cell door slid open. He backed against the wall. Evrain stood in front of him, shielding him.

Symeon's eyes were even redder than usual. They had a glow of madness. "I suppose you thought that the two of you would only have to deal with Imelda and her pathetic little coven," Symeon said, his tone ice cold. "Well, I'm done with sucking up to that bitch. Her caution is just a sign of cowardice. She hasn't the guts to do what needs to be done."

"And you do?" Evrain challenged.

"You'll soon see." Symeon's eyes sparked. His skin was flushed and sweaty. "You thought you could take everything away from me. My power. My influence. My lover." Damon appeared at his shoulder. "As you can see, you were wrong on all counts. You're finished, Evrain. You are both coming with me. We'll soon see what some potent warlock blood can really do." Sparks flew from Symeon's hands, striking Evrain's chest. He dropped to his knees. Damon slipped around him. He grabbed Dominic's arm, holding a blade to his throat, then pushed him toward the door.

Symeon cackled. "Behave yourself, Evrain, and I will make sure that Damon's hand stays steady. Try and escape me and I will not be responsible for the consequences. It would be a shame to mark Dominic's beautiful skin, wouldn't it?" He produced a jeweled dagger. "I can't wait to use this on you." Symeon bent over Evrain, wound a fist into his hair and dragged him upright. He used the dagger to slice the nylon suit from Evrain's body, leaving him bared to the waist. He ran a hand across his chest, viciously pinching a nipple before running his tongue down the side of his face. "You and I are going to have such fun together." He thrust a hand into the overalls and groped him. "I have nothing to lose and it's time you learnt that resisting me is futile. You will regret ever thinking you could defeat me, boy."

"Get your hands off him!" Dominic fought Damon's hold. A burning line across his neck told him that the knife had broken skin.

"Don't fight him, Dominic," Evrain ordered.

"Good advice." Symeon shoved Evrain toward the door. "Bring the puppy, Damon. If he bites, smack his nose."

"Ever heard of karma, Damon? I hope it comes back to bite you in the ass," Dominic whispered. Symeon and Evrain were a few meters ahead. Damon shoved him against the wall.

"Shut your mouth." He winked, then grinned. "Not everything's always as it seems."

For the first time since he'd arrived at the Coven's premises Dominic allowed himself to hope that he and Evrain might just escape with their lives.

Chapter Twelve

Imelda Krenick counted down the minutes until she could return to the young warlock's cell. She prowled the corridors of the office building owned by the Octis Coven under the cover of several shell companies registered in the Caymans. Multiple businesses controlled by Octis members operated out of the tower block in downtown Portland. If anyone ever remarked on the levels of security it was easy enough to cite the dangers of corporate espionage. There was some truth in it. The network of witches in North America was extensive and they were not all allies. Evrain's blood would give her organization a significant advantage over its competitors for many years to come.

She was taking a risk allowing Evrain time alone with his partner but she would prefer to gain his cooperation without violence. If anyone could convince Evrain to donate his blood, it was Dominic Castine.

"It's time, Imelda." One of her assistants approached her.

"Indeed. I'll go to the viewing room first." She walked in the direction of the elevators. She wanted a few minutes to spy on the two young men. Their actions might give her a clue as to how to proceed — with carrot or stick.

Imelda stared at the monitor in the small dark office. She clenched her fists and felt her cheeks begin to heat. For a while she wasn't prepared to accept the fact that the white room was empty. In an uncharacteristic display of temper, she slammed a fist against the table. She thrust her chair back, knocking it over. She twirled on a sharp stiletto heel then swept out of the door, trailed by her assistant.

She made her way to the basement in silence. People she

passed didn't make eye contact or attempt to speak to her. They knew better. When she reached the white room she examined every corner of the bleak space, her assistant shadowing her every move. Other than a couple of spots of blood on the floor, there were no clues. Imelda dipped a finger into one of the spots then tasted it. A few entirely unladylike words hissed from between her crimson painted lips. "This is Dominic's blood. They didn't escape. Someone took them. I'm going to flay Symeon Malus alive." She tapped her foot impatiently. "Get me the video from the last hour," she ordered her assistant. "We may not have been watching them, but we were certainly recording. I want to know everything they said, every word that passed between them. I want confirmation that Malus was involved. There's no possible way he could have gotten both of them out of here without help. When I find out which treacherous bitch was involved, she will wish she hadn't been born."

Imelda returned to her office. She sat stiffly waiting while the video was retrieved and turned on. Fury filled her when she realized Dominic and Evrain had moved away from the camera's field. Much of their conversation was inaudible. "They were whispering, damn it." She could only make out one or two words and they didn't help. She did see the door open, Symeon's arrival and the subsequent exchange between Symeon and Evrain.

If she'd had a weapon to hand, Imelda would have destroyed the monitor. "I should have known that double-crossing bastard was not to be trusted. He's an addict just like any other and not in control of his senses. He might come running back when he needs more of my potion but he's had his last drop. He can kiss goodbye to any further cooperation from me no matter what he promises. I don't intend to wait for something to happen either — we're going to go after him. Vast amounts of time and money went into bringing Evrain Brookes here. I intend to have his blood one way or another. I won't be thwarted by Symeon fucking Malus."

Imelda squared her shoulders and pursed her lips. She could barely hold back her rage. She began snapping out orders and making plans. Her assistants made urgent phone calls and text messages were stabbed into phones as she gathered her resources. "They will all soon know that I am not to be trifled with." The declaration was laced with venom.

* * * *

Dominic and Evrain made their descent to the sub-basement parking garage in the service elevator. Dominic really wanted to wipe the smirk from Symeon's face. The man made gloating an art form. In contrast, Evrain's expression was carefully blank, despite the fact that Symeon was gripping his arm hard enough to bruise and taking every opportunity to touch and grope. Dominic hadn't gotten an opportunity to let him know that Damon was still on their side. He hoped that Damon's presence meant that Nathaniel was also nearby.

There was a black van parked in the far corner of the garage behind a pillar and it was toward this that Damon pushed Dominic. Dominic pretended to stumble. Damon cursed and pressed his curved dagger's wicked blade into Dominic's throat, nicking his skin enough to allow small droplets of blood to trickle down his neck.

"Don't fuck with me, Castine."

Symeon was watching them both.

"I'm not! I stood on a piece of glass…"

Symeon turned his attention back to Evrain, ignoring him. "Sit on the floor, hands on your head. I'll take a look," Damon snapped.

Dominic sat, allowing Damon to inspect the sole of his foot. "We have to get that collar off Evrain," Dominic whispered.

"You think I don't know that? I have the key. I haven't been able to get close enough."

"I have an idea. Give me the key."

Damon hauled him to his feet, using the move to press a small key into Dominic's palm. He grasped it tightly then let Damon lead him toward the van.

Symeon was barely keeping Evrain under control despite his bound hands. He cuffed him hard around the head a couple of times but Evrain ignored the blows and continued to struggle. Dominic guessed he was trying to delay Symeon. Once they were in the van, Gregory and Nathaniel would have much less chance of tracking them down. It was good motivation to fight.

Dominic had a significant height advantage over Damon so with little thought for the damage that Damon's blade might do to his neck he suddenly dropped, twisted and threw the smaller man over his shoulder. Damon's grunt of pain as he hit the concrete floor of the garage made Dominic feel a little guilty but his bruised ass was in a good cause. The knife had been thrown loose from Damon's grip. Dominic scrabbled on the floor to reach it, the rough concrete grazing his knees through the thin nylon overalls. He finally grabbed it. He turned one way then the other to see if Damon was coming after him. Damon was still on the floor, holding his wrist and groaning.

Symeon circled an arm around Evrain's neck, pulling him away from the scuffle. Dominic held the knife up, mesmerized by the glint of the dim garage lighting on the blade. He wasn't so distracted that he didn't take note of Damon climbing unsteadily to his feet. He held the knife out in front of his body then backed toward Evrain.

"Deal with him, Damon," Symeon snarled. "We don't have time for this."

Dominic braced himself. Damon charged toward him. They made contact, Damon driving him back like a footballer in tackle practice. Dominic let the momentum carry him. The two of them crashed into Evrain and Symeon and they all ended up on the ground. Dominic scrambled free first, trying to get a picture of who was where. He still had hold of the key but the knife was gone. Evrain had rolled toward the van. Symeon seemed stunned and was holding his head. Damon lay on the floor, moaning. The knife stuck out of his chest.

Dominic froze. He needed to free Evrain. Once the collar was gone and his hands were free, he would be able to use his power. Symeon would have no chance against him. He needed the knife.

Dominic knelt by Damon's prone form, blocking him from Symeon's view. "Jesus, Damon. What have you done to yourself?" He couldn't see much blood.

"Stab vest. Nathaniel insisted," Damon murmured, keeping his voice low. "Pull the knife out."

"Fuck, you scared me!"

"Hurry up. Symeon won't use his power, he's drained and he hasn't had any potion in twenty-four hours. This is your best chance."

Dominic pulled the knife, which came free easily. Damon screamed and clutched at his chest. He was acting his heart out. Dominic stood, gripping the knife. He stared at Symeon, who was scrambling to his feet. Rather than rushing to his lover's side, Symeon backed even further away, muttering an irritated curse. Dominic took steady paces toward Symeon who, as Damon had predicted, made no attempt to use his power. He had no other weapon that Dominic could see.

"Don't hesitate, Dominic!" Evrain shouted the words even as Symeon made a grab for him. Symeon forced Evrain across the garage so he stood with his back to a wall with Evrain in front of him. Evrain twisted in Symeon's grip, fighting hard.

Dominic was at a loss. This was stalemate and he had no idea what to do next. Symeon had a firm grip on Evrain and though the knife still glinted in his hand, Dominic couldn't see a way of using it without hurting Evrain. Behind him Damon's groans were getting louder.

"Symeon, help me." Damon's words were slurred and

difficult to understand.

Dominic wondered if there was a sliver of compassion in Symeon's psyche that he could appeal to. "He's dying, Symeon. It sounds as if he's bleeding to death and he's going to drown in his own blood if you don't help him."

"Shut your mouth! Damon has never been anything more to me than a convenient piece of ass." He focused his red glare on Dominic. "Now give me that knife, boy, then go and get in the van. Neither of you are going anywhere without me and if we don't move soon Imelda will have people down here looking for us. I'm sure you don't want that. I'm a far better option than that bitch."

The knife in Dominic's hand wavered for just a moment as he thought about the consequences of Imelda getting her hands on Evrain once more.

"What do I do?" he asked urgently, hoping that Evrain would have some kind of inspiration. Evrain's beautiful green-gold eyes flashed but he could only shrug.

"I hate to say it, but we have no choice. We need to get out of this building. Give him the knife, Dominic, there's nothing else you can do." His words said one thing but his expression said something completely different. His eyes bored into Dominic, making his intent absolutely clear. Dominic gave a minute nod of his head to show that he understood and took a couple of steps toward them.

"Not so fast!" Symeon snapped out the words and gave a vicious yank to Evrain's hair. "Throw the knife onto the floor, then turn around and walk slowly toward the van." Dominic made sure his expression was perfect, part desperation, part frustration. He did as he was told and cringed at the metallic clatter of the knife hitting the floor. He avoided Evrain's eyes and turned toward the van, praying that Evrain would not be hurt by what was going to happen next. Dominic kept walking, nudging Damon's body with his foot as he passed. Damon gave a faint moan of acknowledgement.

Behind him he heard a sharp scream and whirled back to

see Evrain twist violently from Symeon's grip then throw himself forward on to the ground. Fingers slicked with blood grasped for the abandoned knife. He had launched himself forward with no thought for his bound hands or the fact that he was still shirtless, and as he rolled Dominic could see severe grazing up his arm and across a pale shoulder. His bare feet scrabbled for purchase as the knife skittered just out of reach.

Dominic turned and ran as fast as he could back toward them. Symeon had dived at Evrain's legs and was clawing his way along his body, pinning him to the concrete floor. Dominic reached them in seconds. He grabbed a fistful of white hair then pulled. Symeon screamed but didn't let go of Evrain, so Dominic yanked again and this time Symeon rolled away. Evrain still hadn't managed to grasp the knife so Dominic picked it up. He sliced through the plastic binding connecting the cuffs around Evrain's outstretched hands. He winced at the damage that was left beneath the ties, but Evrain looked up at him and grinned. Adrenaline flooding his system, Dominic grinned back. He displayed the small key in his hand. There was a key-shaped indentation on his palm where he'd been gripping it so tightly. Fumbling a bit in his haste, he unlocked the collar around Evrain's neck. Evrain pulled it apart then threw it, Frisbee style, across the garage floor. He struggled to his knees.

"Start the van," he urged. "Damon probably has the keys. I'll deal with Symeon." He scrambled toward the other warlock. A blast of power sent Symeon spinning toward the wall where he banged his head, slumping into unconsciousness.

Dominic searched around for Damon, who appeared next to him.

"I have the keys." He jangled them. "Can we get out of here now?"

"What the…" Evrain stood. "I thought you were…I mean you had a knife sticking out of you. Didn't you?"

"He's with us," Dominic said. "Sorry — didn't get a chance

to tell you."

Keys in hand, Damon ran to the van, yanked open the door and started it.

By the wall, Symeon moaned.

"Fuck, he's coming round." Evrain gave Dominic a push. "Van. Now!"

Dominic ran to the vehicle. He jumped in next to Damon. Leaning from the open door he yelled, "Let's go, Evrain!"

Out of the corner of his eye Dominic thought he saw a flash of flame and when Damon pulled forward he could see that Evrain was taking full advantage of access to his power. He wasn't channeling — this was uncontrolled wild magic. His eyes were glowing, green as a cat's, and his dark hair was blowing in a supernatural wind. Dust was flying around his ankles. As he brought his arms up he laughed when the pipes above his head burst and water came flooding down. Symeon cowered against the wall, his fingers flickering rapidly, but there was little he could do against such enormous power. In the end, half drowned by water, harassed by wind and dust, all he could do was cover his head and whimper.

Dominic hoped that Evrain had his abilities under control. Symeon must have been praying for his life. Evrain was frightening, standing amidst the elements, blood-streaked arms held aloft, his lips murmuring words of power as he threw water, wind and fire around the basement. Dominic understood his fury but he couldn't let it continue. He scrambled out of the van and got as close as he dared. The wind buffeted him so hard he could barely remain upright.

"Cut the pyrotechnics and get in the damned van, Evrain!" He yelled in Evrain's direction. For a few moments Dominic thought that he was going to be ignored, but Evrain stilled and his gaze flicked toward Dominic. He gave a slight nod. He lowered his arms and stared at Symeon's pathetic figure huddled in the corner. Evrain took half a step toward him and Dominic wondered if things were going to get bloody. Evrain didn't speak. He deliberately turned his back on Symeon—a calculated insult—then walked over to Dominic. Holding out his arms, he remained still until Dominic walked into his embrace, accepting a thorough, passionate kiss.

"We need to go."

"Sure. Let's get out of here," Evrain agreed. "Imelda can deal with what's left of Symeon."

Dominic got back into the van, sliding across to sit next to Damon. Evrain climbed in next to him before slamming the door shut.

"Kissing? Really? You think we have time for that?" Damon snarked. He put the van in drive then headed for the exit ramp.

"For someone who was just supposedly stabbed, you're remarkably talkative," Evrain replied. "And opinionated. Brat."

Dominic glanced from Evrain to Damon and back again. They were both grinning. He sighed. "Can we please just get out of here? I really don't want to spend any more time in Imelda's company and she can't be far behind us."

Damon drove toward the exit door but it didn't open.

"Fuck. She's locked down the building. Evrain—can you do something about it?"

"My pleasure."

This time Dominic felt the discomfort as Evrain channeled his power. He gathered the air into a spinning whirlwind then threw it against the door. The metal panel blasted outward. Damon revved the engine then tore up the ramp. He skidded into the street and the van filled with the smell of burning rubber.

Emerging from the underground parking garage into the light of a sunny afternoon was blinding. Dominic blinked into the sun and tried to get his bearings, surrounded as they were by anonymous office blocks.

"You were right," Evrain said. "We're in Portland."

"You didn't know?" Damon asked.

"I was unconscious when I was brought here," Evrain

explained. "Dominic was drugged too. We made an educated guess."

Damon glanced in the rear view mirror. "We don't have a tail yet." He took one hand off the wheel to grope in his pocket. He tossed a phone toward Dominic. "Can you call Nathaniel?"

"Sure."

"There's no password. His is the only number. It's just a cheap burner phone he got me in case I ran into trouble. I wasn't able to get word to him about the location of the building but he's probably not far away." He wended his way through the traffic and eventually found the route out of town.

Dominic handed the phone to Evrain. "Probably best you speak to Nathaniel. I'll see if there's anything in the back of the van that you can wear." He scrambled over the seat into the rear cargo space.

Evrain dialed the single number in Damon's directory.

"Nathaniel?" He put the loudspeaker on.

"Yes. Evrain, is that you? Where's Damon?"

"He's driving. He gave me his phone."

"And Dominic? You're all okay?"

"We're all intact. Damon's on the list for best actor at this year's Oscars."

"We'll reconvene at your place. I'll let Gregory and Coryn know. We need to employ some delaying tactics on Imelda and her cronies. That might get us some respite to plan our next move."

"Don't have too much fun." Evrain hung up.

"What are they gonna do?" Damon asked.

"Cause some mayhem, I imagine."

Dominic clambered into the front seat. "Here. I found an old workman's jacket in the back." He wrapped it around Evrain's bare shoulders. It wasn't that cold but Evrain was shivering. "Are you okay?" Dominic's voice was edged with concern as he took in the black hollows beneath Evrain's eyes and the blood streaking his hands and arms.

"I'll survive. It's all my fault we're in this mess, so don't waste your sympathy on me."

Dominic gave an exasperated sigh. "Don't be ridiculous. It's hardly your fault that a coven of psychotic witches and a junkie warlock are after your blood." He giggled, a little hysterical. "That sounds insane."

"I'm glad you can see the humorous side of this, Dominic." Evrain glared at him through narrowed eyes. "We'll see how funny you find it when I lock you up at Hornbeam and never let you out again." He rested his head against the cracked red vinyl of his seat and closed his eyes. "And I haven't forgotten your reference to my 'pyrotechnics' either. Cheeky brat. At the very least that merits a spanking."

Damon gave a snort of laughter. Dominic's face heated. He kept his eyes on the road. When he risked casting a nervous, sidelong look at Evrain he had fallen asleep. Dominic breathed a sigh of relief. Hopefully by the time Evrain woke up he would have forgotten his threat.

"You're in soooo much trouble," Damon said, giggling.

"And when I tell Nathaniel how you risked your life for us, you will be too. I'll bet that stab vest was for protection only. I doubt Nathaniel sanctioned you actually taking a knife in the chest."

"Um, there's no need to mention all the details, is there?" Damon made puppy eyes. "My butt doesn't need decoration." He shivered. "Though it might not be all bad."

"Way too much information, Damon. Just drive."

"Spoilsport."

"What are you, three?"

"We're the same age aren't we, or close enough?"

"Birth certificate says one thing, your mouth says another."

"Hey, we're bickering. That means we must be friends."

"God help me." Dominic wished Evrain was awake.

The rest of the drive home was uneventful. Dominic controlled his tiredness and let Evrain sleep. Every now and again he cast a sideways glance at the dark head wedged against the van window, eyelids flickering as Evrain dreamed. There were smudges on his face and the faint marks of developing bruises around his neck where Symeon had held him and presumably where the collar had been tight against his flesh. The filthy workman's jacket hung open to expose part of his smooth chest, which was rising and falling gently. Dominic brushed at the warm salt tears that welled in the corners of his eyes. Evrain looked so vulnerable and Dominic hated that he had been hurt. He thumped one hand against his seat, beating out the rhythm of his frustration in time to the low rumbling of the van's engine. To his relief, Damon kept his mouth firmly closed.

The light was beginning to fade by the time Damon parked the van at the end of the lane leading to Hornbeam Cottage. He switched off the ignition with a sigh — of what appeared to be — relief, turning to press his forehead against the glass next to him.

"The others aren't back yet." He squinted into the trees. "I can't see anything suspicious but then I probably wouldn't."

"Symeon wasn't in any condition to come after us by the time Evrain had finished with him," Dominic said. "If Gregory and Nathaniel are dealing with Imelda then we have some time."

Evrain began to stir. Dominic placed a reassuring hand on his thigh.

"We're home. How do you feel?"

Green-gold eyes flickered open and regarded him with piercing scrutiny.

"I feel like taking you over my knee and spanking the disobedience out of you. That's how I feel. In fact I've been dreaming about it."

Dominic stared at him. Heat built in his cheeks and his cock jerked. "You really are an ungrateful bastard, aren't you?"

"If things are going to get stormy, I'm out of here." Damon almost fell out of the van in his hurry to escape.

Dominic gave Evrain a glare he didn't mean then

followed Damon. He slammed the door behind him then leaned against the side of the van. Seconds later, Evrain joined him. He had discarded the borrowed jacket and was bare-chested. The wounds on his arms and around his wrists looked stark against his pale skin and his midnight hair was in wild disarray. He braced one arm each side of Dominic's shoulders and leaned toward him.

"Do you want me to be grateful that you put yourself at risk? Grateful that you suffered so much pain for me? Grateful that I was such a fucking idiot that I put us both in danger?"

Dominic hardly heard the words. He was too busy trying not to drool at the sight of the muscles flexing in Evrain's arms and chest. He made an effort and focused. "Was that your attempt at an apology? You need to rethink your..." Dominic's protests were cut off as his lips were crushed by a forceful kiss. An insistent tongue pushed its way into his mouth, probing deeply, until he thought he would run out of breath. Evrain encircled his wrist with long slender fingers then tugged him away from the van and down the path to the cottage.

Intent on his destination, Evrain didn't speak again. Even with his feet bare, he moved quickly and Dominic found himself half-running to avoid falling. He felt strange — half scared, half excited, his cock now swollen so much it rubbed against his overalls. Evrain was so intense, no doubt driven by a basic need to re-establish his dominance, but surely he wouldn't follow through with his threat.

The cottage was empty. Shadow was nowhere to be seen and there was no sign of Gregory, Coryn or any indication that unwelcome intruders had gotten past the wards. The pots and pans used to brew the agrimony solution sat on the draining board, bringing back painful memories.

"Evrain, stop!" Dominic resisted his pulling. "We have company, remember."

Damon, who had tailed them through the door, wiggled his fingers in a small wave. "Don't stop on my account.

Really. I'm kinda enjoying the show."

"Can I fry him? Please, can I?" Evrain wiggled his fingers.

"No!" Dominic and Damon spoke at the same time, though Damon's 'no' was more of a yelp while Dominic's was a reprimand.

"Fuck." Evrain threw himself into the armchair next to the fireplace. It was already laid. He gestured toward the logs, which burst into flame.

Dominic dropped to his knees next to him. "The others will be back soon. I want to be with you too — more than you could possibly know — but later, when we're alone and we have time to enjoy each other. Okay?"

"Okay." Evrain pouted but his lips twitched into a smile. "Sorry."

"No you're not."

"No, I'm not. We could shove Damon outside and lock the door?"

"He just helped save your ass, Evrain. Be nice."

"I'm not very good at nice."

"Why don't you take a shower then put some proper clothes on? Much as I like having you sitting around half naked, you're filthy. Damon and I will see what we can pull together for a meal of sorts."

"You need to shower and change too," Evrain wheedled. "You could come join me."

"I could, but I don't think that's a good idea."

"It's an excellent idea, but I'll let you off this once. I'm starving." Evrain hauled himself from his seat, fatigue apparent in his obvious effort. "That spanking is only on hold until later." He sauntered toward the stairs, casting a knowing glance back over his shoulder.

Dominic got to his feet, groaning at his aching muscles. Damon was perched on the edge of the kitchen table, swinging his legs.

"You really have your hands full with him, don't you?" Damon grinned. "Warlocks are all so dommy."

"Evrain isn't cruel like Symeon though." Dominic felt the

need to defend his lover.

"No one, warlock or not, is as bad as Symeon. Nathaniel is totally different."

"You really like him, don't you?"

Damon nodded. "He's given me a proper contract. He hasn't fucked me even though I wish he would." Damon sounded wistful.

"He's giving you time. It's not that long since you were with Symeon. It will take you a while to get over what that bastard did to you."

"True. But I kinda feel that I need Nathaniel to give me better memories."

"Then tell him," Dominic said.

"Maybe." Damon hopped off the table. "Now, what are we going to cook? Do you two even keep groceries in the house?"

"Of course we do." Dominic rolled his eyes. "There are a couple tubs of stew in the freezer. We can put them in a big pot on the stove. I know how to make herb dumplings."

"You do?" Damon licked his lips with a slurping sound. "I might just have to move in here."

"Evrain would roast you within a week." Dominic retrieved the storage boxes of stew from the freezer then emptied them into a big pan. He gathered the ingredients for the dumplings.

"Can I help?" Damon bounced on his toes. "I need to do something, I'm still a bit hyper."

Dominic laughed. "Can you rub butter into flour?"

"Sure can."

Dominic roughly measured out the ingredients. "If you do that I'll pick some fresh parsley from the garden." He padded to the door where he pulled on an old pair of boots. He couldn't wait to get out of the scratchy overalls which were all he wore, but he could put up with the ridiculous outfit for a while longer. He opened the door and almost fell as a rocket-powered ball of black fur barreled into his legs. "Hey, Shadow. Where have you been?" He scooped the cat into his arms. Purring vibrated through his chest. "Happy to see me, huh?" He cuddled Shadow, absorbing her warmth. "Evrain's back. He's upstairs." Shadow squirmed until he let her down. She immediately shot toward the stairs.

"Easy to see where the fur ball's loyalties lie," Damon called.

"No comment." Dominic stomped outside to find herbs.

In the garden he automatically checked around. He hated feeling so vulnerable even behind the cottage wards. There was no sign of anyone beyond the garden boundary from what he could see and things felt…normal. The birds were singing. A light breeze rustled the trees. He relaxed a little but didn't waste any time gathering the herbs he needed. He was returning to the cottage when he heard voices and laughter coming down the path. He recognized Gregory's smooth tones and Coryn's chuckle. He waited next to the door for them all to arrive.

"That's an interesting outfit, Dominic," Gregory said. "And why are you outside?"

Dominic waved his bunch of herbs in response.

"Where's Damon?" Nathaniel seemed on edge.

"Damon's safe inside helping with dinner. Evrain is upstairs getting changed. Even Shadow's back safe and sound."

"Then why don't we all go inside?" That was Felix, bringing up the rear, a broad grin on his face.

Dominic led the way, feeling more than a bit self-conscious in his overalls. He put the herbs on the table but couldn't give Damon any more instruction because he had flung himself into Nathaniel's arms. Coryn put his arm around Dominic's shoulders.

"Well done."

"We were lucky. Damon helped a lot."

"We'll save all our stories for later when we're all here, otherwise we'll be repeating ourselves. There's a lot to discuss."

Evrain appeared at the bottom of the stairs. His hair

appeared even darker than usual because it was still damp. His skin was pale, making the bruises on his skin stand out. Gregory went to him, grasped his shoulders then pulled him into a hug.

"I'm glad you're safe."

"I brought it on myself," Evrain murmured.

"No. You were careless, but things would have come to a head eventually. Don't beat yourself up."

Coryn patted Dominic's back. "Why don't you go and freshen up? Damon and I can finish off here, then the food should be ready by the time you're done."

"That would be great, thanks, Coryn." Dominic crossed the room. His fingers brushed Evrain's as he passed. Fire flashed in Evrain's eyes, holding a promise for later. Dominic was grateful to escape to the bathroom for a few minutes of solitude.

After a rapid clean-up and fresh clothes, Dominic felt a whole lot better. He was tired but eager to hear what had happened to the others. He did take the time to dry his hair before re-joining his friends around the kitchen table. To his surprise, Shadow was ensconced on Damon's lap, purring with significant decibels. Damon was stroking her and giggling.

"Just a few minutes for the dumplings to cook, then we can eat," Coryn relayed from his position next to the stove. "There's a mug of coffee for you on the table, Dominic."

Dominic took the free seat next to Evrain. "So, can we expect Imelda to come knocking any time soon?"

"Not likely," Nathaniel said. "Seems there was a small earthquake in Portland today. There's a significant crevice in the road outside her building. She won't be going anywhere for a while. I would imagine the foundations will have to be checked too. Her sad little potions won't be able to deal with that." He gave Gregory a conspiratorial wink.

"It got rather squally too." Gregory grinned. "High winds took out all the communications equipment on the roof of that building and quite a few others."

"You two had some fun then?" Dominic chuckled.

"We did. Felix did good work identifying the locations of all Octis-owned buildings," Gregory said. "Then we used our strengths to best effect."

"Won't the authorities be wondering about all these weird natural phenomena occurring at the same time?" Dominic asked.

"I'm sure they will. It's always a pleasure to give the scientific community something to puzzle over for a while. In the meantime, Imelda Krenick will be far too busy to chase after us for a while."

"What about Symeon?" Evrain asked. "I left him alive. Well, sort of. He was a blubbering mess by the time we left."

"Who knows?" Gregory shrugged. "None of us saw him so we can only assume Imelda got him. If he did manage to get away from her, it will take him some time to recover, especially if he's cut off from Octis' potion."

Dominic wasn't happy with the idea that Symeon might still be on the loose but he was too tired to care that much.

"Let's eat." Coryn distributed plates of stew and aromatic dumplings. Even Shadow got a small dish on the floor, which she wasted no time in abandoning Damon in favor of. "Then Gregory can bring Evrain up to speed with everything that happened after he was captured. Evrain can tell us all about what happened to him and Damon can recount his day with Symeon."

"Sounds like a recipe for indigestion to me," Felix commented. "Food first. Talk later."

Nobody protested and the sounds of contented munching filled the room.

Chapter Thirteen

Evrain pulled Dominic up the stairs and into their bedroom. He knew he was being rough but his patience had run out some time ago. They were finally alone and his only imperative was to remind Dominic who he belonged to. He propelled Dominic toward the bed.

"It's about bloody time I got you in here. I thought the others would never leave." He gave Dominic a light shove so he fell backward onto the bed.

"We owe them everything."

"But I owe you most of all. What Gregory put you through was inhuman. I'm not sure I can forgive him for that." He unfastened Dominic's brown leather belt then slid it from its loops.

"There's nothing to forgive. Gregory came up with the only plan that could work. I volunteered to be part of it. He wouldn't have done anything without my consent, Evrain."

"In that he and I are in agreement. Consent is non-negotiable." Evrain pulled Dominic's jeans down his legs. He cast them into a corner.

"You've absorbed the agrimony. Your blood is useless to the Octis Coven now — or any other coven for that matter."

"But we got away without Imelda discovering that. This isn't over. But in the meantime I have to punish you for putting yourself at risk."

"You're not really going to spank me, are you?" Dominic pushed Evrain's fumbling fingers away from his shirt then undid his own buttons.

Evrain groped Dominic's cock through his shorts. "You're hard just thinking about it, aren't you?"

"No! That's not why… It's because you're touching me."

"I need to spank you. You need to be spanked. That's all there is to it."

"That argument doesn't work for me." Dominic squirmed away. He retreated further up the bed but Evrain grabbed his ankle and pulled him back.

"I could tie you down and flog you instead."

"No! You wouldn't dare." Dominic flipped over onto his knees. He attempted to crawl away but Evrain clambered onto the bed and straddled him, pushing him flat into the mattress.

"A compromise then. You keep absolutely still and I won't fetch my best flogger from the closet."

"Fine." Dominic grabbed a pillow, thumped it a few times then shoved it beneath his head.

Evrain smiled. He might not fetch the flogger but he hadn't placed any other restrictions on himself. Dominic needed to learn to be more specific. Taking a few moments to remove his top, Evrain admired Dominic's lithe body stretched out on the bed. There was no sign of the silvery green tattoos that had graced his skin. They had been beautiful designs. Evrain wondered if he could persuade Dominic to get some more permanent ink. Some protective sigils perhaps.

He pictured how the symbols might look whilst fetching a roll of bondage tape from the toy box in the closet. He also extracted a pair of scissors from his washbag on the dresser. He cut a length of the shiny black tape. He liked its tactile nature and the fact that it left no sticky residue on Dominic's skin.

"Legs together." He chuckled. "Now there's a phrase I don't use often."

Dominic twisted his head so he could give him a dubious look. Before he could work out Evrain's intention, Evrain slipped the tape beneath Dominic's ankles then wound it around them in several tight loops.

"Hey!" Dominic started to struggle just a little. Evrain gave him a sharp smack across the ass.

"Be still. Put your arms above your head."

Damon stretched out with a huff. Evrain used more tape to bind his wrists together then attached them to the headboard with enough slack that he could turn over if Evrain desired it.

"No warlock tricks?" Dominic asked.

"Sometimes it's good to be a bit more...hands on." Evrain used the scissors to cut down one side of Dominic's shorts. He flipped the resulting flap of fabric aside, exposing one smooth cheek.

"What are you doing, Evrain?"

"Uncovering my property." He snipped the other seam. There was something satisfying and intensely erotic about seeing Dominic's ass partially covered by ragged underwear. He pulled the scrap of fabric from beneath Dominic's body, leaving him naked. Evrain couldn't resist kneading the muscled cheeks he had exposed. He had to force his finger between them to rub Dominic's hole. Dominic moaned.

"Maybe I shouldn't have tied your legs quite so tightly," Evrain mused. "Still, you look so pretty like this." He stripped off his pants and underwear, enjoying the cool air on his overheated skin. "Bring your knees up. I need better access to that gorgeous ass."

"Fucking megalomaniac." Dominic had to engage in a kind of caterpillar crawl to get into position but ended up as Evrain wanted him, head down and ass up.

"Perfect." Evrain flexed his fingers. "You know you deserve this, don't you?" It wasn't really a question, just an absolute statement of fact. Dominic blushed.

"There's no need to feel ashamed of what your body craves." Evrain rested his hand on the small of Dominic's back. "Do you understand why I have to punish you?"

"For rescuing your sorry ass?"

Evrain gave Dominic's butt a soft pat. "Try again." Dominic pushed back against his palm. He smiled.

"For putting myself at risk."

"That's one reason."

"Then I should be punishing you!"

"That wouldn't be nearly as much fun for either of us, now would it? What else?"

"I have no fucking idea." Dominic squirmed but Evrain allowed him no leverage to rise. "Stop it! You can't do this."

"I think I can. Much as I love to hear you beg, that sounded half-hearted. I don't think you meant it." Evrain punctuated his response with several hard slaps. For Evrain the feeling of his open palm connecting with the smooth, firm flesh of Dominic's perfect ass was incredibly erotic. He knew that he was pushing boundaries, but he also knew that if he wanted to Dominic could stop what was happening at any time. "You also allowed other men to see you naked. To tie you down."

"It was necessary," Dominic snarled. "You think I enjoyed it?"

"Then you undressed in front of Imelda Krenick. I think you enjoy being naked, Dominic. I should confiscate your clothes and keep you that way all the time. Perhaps then you wouldn't get up to so much mischief."

Dominic groaned. "There's no reasoning with you, is there? You don't need to make up excuses to spank me. Just get on with it!"

"I thought a sense of injustice might make it even better for you." Evrain chuckled. He could see how aroused Dominic was. His cock was rigid, the silvery gleam of pre-cum evident on its head. "You're not to come until I allow it." He landed a firm blow right in the center of Dominic's ass.

"I'm too close," Dominic gasped.

Evrain glanced around the room. His gaze rested on a copper dish on the dresser. Normally used for loose change or keys, it was currently empty. He picked it up then channeled his power, manipulating the molecules of metal into a new shape. When he was done the smooth copper ring had no joins.

"Why are you channeling, Evrain? What are you up to?"

Evrain slipped his hand beneath Dominic's body. He placed the large ring around the base of his balls then muttered a few more words. The metal contracted and spread, then split into a set of joined rings forming a cage that would act as a very effective chastity device. Dominic ducked his head to peer beneath his body. "What have you done? I hope you know how to get that off."

"I told you to research the gates of hell, didn't I? I never got the chance to go shopping but this is just as good — and the copper looks beautiful against your skin. Now you can focus on your punishment and not be concerned about coming without permission," Evrain said, feeling smug.

"You're too kind."

"I know. I need to cultivate more a of a wicked warlock persona. Much sexier." As if to illustrate his intentions he began to spank Dominic, landing a series of hard blows, his palm cupped. He kept up a steady rhythm, never striking the same place twice. Dominic's initial yelps faded and his muscles relaxed. Evrain stopped when his hand began to sting. He admired the light red flush that blossomed over Dominic's ass and thighs.

"God, that looks delicious." Evrain grinned and smoothed sore flesh tenderly. "How are you doing?"

"How do you think?" Dominic sounded dreamy.

"I think you're a pain slut and you're floating on a cloud of happiness about now." Evrain snipped the tape binding Dominic's ankles then tapped his calf, encouraging him to spread his legs. Dominic complied. He was breathing hard but seemed almost to be in a trance. "I adore you like this. So trusting. So utterly at my mercy."

Dominic answered with a needy whimper. Evrain grabbed the jar of lube. He slicked his middle finger then pushed into the small, tight entrance that beckoned to him so temptingly. He wiggled his finger and was rewarded with a contented sigh.

"You want to come, don't you, sweetheart?" Evrain

crooked his finger, seeking Dominic's prostate. "Not yet. I feel an overwhelming need to torture you some more." Clambering onto the bed, Evrain got into position behind Dominic. He didn't want to give him time to come down from the endorphin high he must have been riding. He slathered lubrication over his cock, using too much in his eagerness. He pressed against Dominic's entrance then thrust forward in one smooth motion. Dominic cursed, but it was a cry of pleasure rather than pain. Evrain grasped his narrow hips hard enough to leave the bruises he loved to see on Dominic's skin.

"I'm going to mark you, inside and out. Make you mine." He thrust himself forward again and again. He grabbed some of Dominic's hair, yanking his head back, getting the purchase he needed to drive deeper. The urge to claim, to possess, flooded him. "Turn over, love. Want to look into your eyes when I come."

Dominic mumbled a complaint but shifted onto his back. Evrain gave the tape binding Dominic's wrists a quick check to make sure the change of position hadn't tightened it too much. Content that Dominic's circulation was unimpaired, Evrain shoved his knees back, bending him double. He wanted his cock back inside Dominic's grasping heat but paused a moment to admire his lover. Dominic's hair was a wild mess, his cheeks flushed and eyes bright. In its copper prison, his cock strained angrily. Evrain gave Dominic's balls a squeeze, eliciting a half-scream. He grinned and plunged deep into Dominic's channel, spearing him with aggressive thrusts. Despite all his intentions to make Dominic wait as long as possible, Evrain found he could hold back no longer. His back arched and he spurted hot seed into Dominic's tight channel.

He wasn't sure how he managed to maintain the presence of mind to channel enough to release Dominic's cock from the copper cuff, but he did. The release of pressure was enough to push Dominic over the edge. He spent with a few shuddering gasps, Evrain still inside him.

When they separated, Dominic shunted a few inches sideways. A tumult of conflicting emotions played across his face. Evrain collapsed next to him. He stroked a lock of hair away from Dominic's eyes.

"I love you."

"You spanked me." Dominic closed his eyes. "My ass is burning with enough heat that I won't be able to forget it for a while either."

"Good. I want you to feel me for days."

"I could have resisted."

"You could. Of course you could, but you didn't. You stayed there, displayed for me. It was so fucking hot I almost came just looking at you."

"You did?"

"Of course." Evrain trailed a finger down the firm planes of Dominic's chest. "Your submission is a thing of beauty. My hand connecting with your backside doesn't just make *your* ass burn, you know. It sets my cock on fire. Every stroke sends jolts of pleasure through my entire body." Evrain thought Dominic needed to hear that confession. He was clearly going through some conflicting emotions.

"I should be angry with you. You humiliated me. But all I feel is love." He pulled a pillow over his face. "Fuck, fuck, fuck." He growled the words into the pillow.

"I think we just did that." Evrain stroked his stomach, enjoying the twitch of muscles beneath the skin. "That wasn't about humiliating you, you must know that. It was about pleasure for both of us." He gripped Dominic's flaccid cock then gave it a gentle squeeze.

"Hey! Haven't you tormented me enough?" Dominic stayed hidden beneath his pillow.

"Never. You could have stopped me at any time but you didn't. Doesn't that tell you something about what we both needed?"

Dazzling blue eyes set in a very flushed face appeared from beneath the pillow. "Maybe I'm not quite ready to admit it."

"Well, when you are, let me know and I'll give you another reminder." Evrain smirked. He continued to stroke and play, then he dipped his head to lap at Dominic's hard pink nipples.

"What are we going to do, Evrain? We can't stay hidden here forever, however nice it would be." The sadness in Dominic's voice was evident. "I want something close to a normal life."

"You really know how to ruin a moment, don't you?" Evrain slumped back with a sigh. "We both need a decent night's sleep. In the morning, I'll talk to Gregory. First we need to take a shower. Come on." He tugged on a lock of hair.

"What do you mean, come on?"

"I intend to have my wicked way with you...again" — Evrain brushed the back of his hand over Dominic's reviving erection — "and you are clearly in the mood, so get that beautiful ass into the shower and brace yourself."

* * * *

After a restless night's sleep, Evrain was grateful Dominic had had the presence of mind to defrost bread and bacon the night before. Bacon sandwiches and coffee did wonders to improve his mood. So did watching Dominic shift in his seat.

"Would you like a cushion, love?" Evrain decided that risking his life was worth it for the expression on Dominic's face.

"You spanked me then fucked me. Twice. It's hardly surprising that I'm a bit tender, is it? I don't need you bringing it to my attention either. I'm quite aware of how I feel." Shadow jumped onto his lap then began kneading his thighs, clearly adding to the pressure on his sensitized behind. "Oh, for fuck's sake. This is a conspiracy." He glared at the cat, who stared back at him unblinking. Dominic gave in first. "If you bring me the first aid box, I'll dig out some salve for your wrists. And my ass." He whispered the last sentence under his breath but Evrain heard him anyway.

Evrain went to the cupboard under the sink. He hauled out a wooden crate then carried it across to the table. "Calling this a box is a criminal understatement," he said.

"Agatha did like to be prepared for every eventuality," Dominic replied, peering into the cavernous depths. He started to unload the contents onto the table. "Will I need dressings or just the salve?"

Evrain examined his wrists. The cuts weren't deep and they were healing nicely. The grazes on his arms were sore but didn't need covering either. "Just the salve. And if there's some arnica in there, that would be good. The bruises on my neck really ache."

Dominic rummaged around searching for the salve and anything that resembled arnica. The jars and bottles he lined up on the table looked as if they'd come from an early nineteenth century apothecary's shop.

"Belladonna," Dominic read a label. "We could poison half the town with what's in this box."

"Could come in handy then. I'm going to call Gregory."

"Okay. I hope he and Coryn slept better than we did."

Evrain dialed Gregory's number then put the phone on speaker so Dominic could hear. It rang quite a few times before Gregory picked up.

Evrain was still furious that Gregory had used Dominic in the way he had. He blamed his godfather for convincing Dominic to have the magical agrimony painted on his body. He knew how painful the magic must have been and was annoyed that Gregory had made no apologies for what he had done. He resolved to keep his thoughts to himself.

"Good morning, Evrain. Still angry with me?"

Evrain sighed. "Sometimes I think you're a mind-reader, not a warlock. Yes, I'm still mad at you." He rolled his eyes. Dominic grinned.

"Good. The emotion will keep you sharp. He agreed to it, Evrain. He loves you and he wanted to do it for you. Just accept it and move on. We need to focus on the future. How are you both?"

"A bit bruised and battered. We didn't sleep that well. But we're alive. That has to be a plus." He paced up and down as he spoke. "How about you—everything okay at the hotel?"

"I own it. Everything is perfect. Coryn and I have just had a very pleasant breakfast with Nathaniel and Felix. I've also spoken to your boss. Well, the CEO of your company actually. I told him we have some urgent family issues to deal with and that you needed to take a few days' vacation time."

"Thank you. It hadn't even occurred to me that my sudden absence might be noticed and I need my job. I don't want to get fired."

"I told him the circumstances were exceptional."

"You could hardly tell him the truth. You didn't mention Damon. Isn't he with you?"

"Damon, I understand, is having some quiet time. Yesterday's events left him a little…overexcited. Nathaniel felt the need to calm him down some."

"Don't be too hard on him." Evrain could hardly believe he was sticking up for Damon. "Without him we'd probably be at Symeon's mercy and I'd be a few pints short of a full quota."

"Nathaniel is aware of that. Trust me, he understands what Damon needs."

"Okay." Evrain sighed. "So where do we go from here? Your plan worked to some extent because my blood is now useless to Octis, but they're unaware of the taint. Imelda is not going to be happy we escaped. She's not going to stop hunting me. I doubt Symeon will give up either once he's recovered enough."

"I agree and so does Nathaniel. You're too much of a temptation."

"That I agree with," Dominic contributed.

Evrain pressed his lips together to prevent a laugh

escaping.

"We need to put an end to this problem once and for all," Gregory said. "I know we'd be taking a risk but the only way I can see to do that is to meet with Imelda face to face."

"I don't like it, but I think you're right. It's probably the only way to get her off my back." Evrain avoided making eye contact with Dominic.

"But this time it will be on our terms. I could give her some of your blood myself, but she would never believe that it was yours. She needs to see it extracted personally. I will arrange a meeting. With Nathaniel and me there you will be well protected."

"It's not me that I'm worried about and you know it, Gregory. If we do this, Dominic will have to be there too. Putting him in danger again isn't acceptable."

Dominic tapped on the table to attract his attention then raised his eyebrows in question.

"Hold on, Gregory, I think Dominic has something to say."

"Can you think of a better way to resolve this, Evrain, because I can't?" Dominic looked so serious. "You have to let me help. It affects both of us, not just you. We need to end this situation and we need to end it decisively. It isn't just your choice to make."

"I can see that you still need a little more educating about who makes the decisions around here," Evrain muttered. "It will be my pleasure to teach you, but much as I hate to admit it, this time you're right. I think I'm just trying to find a reason not to go ahead."

"If you two have quite finished?" Gregory sounded amused.

"Okay, Gregory, I don't like it, but I can't see any other way. Arrange the meeting. Let us know where we need to be and we'll be there."

"Stay at home, Evrain. No wandering. This probably won't take long. Imelda will be very keen to meet. If she doesn't pull this off she'll lose her power base at Octis."

"I'd prefer not to be a prisoner in my own home for too long. I want to get this over with." Evrain realized he sounded a bit petulant. "I'm sorry, Gregory. I'm just worried."

"Dear boy, I know you are. We will bring all this to a conclusion as soon as possible. In the meantime, try to relax."

"Sure. We'll talk later." He disconnected the call then turned to Dominic. "What else can we do?" He grabbed Dominic's hand, squeezing it lightly.

Dominic shrugged. "Nothing but wait."

"Soon this will be over and we can get on with our lives, I'm sorry I've dragged you into it all."

"Take your top off."

"That wasn't the response I expected." Evrain raised an eyebrow.

"I finally found the right balm and I want to apply it to your wounds without getting it on your clothes."

"You're not just trying to change the subject?" Evrain stripped off his shirt. Dominic began to apply ointment to a cut around one wrist.

"I'm here because I want to be, Evrain. I love you. Every weird, witchy piece of you. Now damn well keep still." He went back to administering first aid, ignoring the glare Evrain shot at him.

"I'm fighting a losing battle with you, aren't I?" Evrain scowled. "How many times am I going to have to paddle your ass before you accept who's in charge? What happened to the shy gardener I fell for?"

"He's still right here. I only feel confident to say what I feel around you. And as for who's in charge, I can be as stubborn as you are. I'm going to take some convincing. Shadow, you're going to have to move. I need to stand up."

Shadow gave an indignant yowl as she was displaced. She stalked toward the fire. "We're almost out of tuna, you know," Dominic called after her. She stuck her tail in the air and ignored him. "I swear that cat is the feline version

of your grandmother. Aggie liked to get her own way too."
He slathered Evrain's grazes with balm.

"Runs in the family." Evrain stood still while Dominic
treated his injuries.

"Don't I know it." Dominic applied arnica to the bruises
around Evrain's neck.

"That's cold!"

"Baby."

"You know…the nurse thing is kinda hot."

Dominic banged the lid shut on the first aid crate. "Leave
your shirt off until the ointments soak in."

Invading Dominic's personal space, Evrain pressed
against him. "If I'm half naked, you should be too." He
encircled Dominic with his arms, resting his hands on the
swell of his ass. "Neither of us slept well. I think we should
go back to bed for a nap."

"A nap?" Dominic sounded suspicious.

"Let's call it an active snooze." Evrain hustled Dominic
toward the stairs. On the armchair next to the fire, Shadow
purred in feline contentment.

* * * *

Spending the morning with Dominic wrapped in his
arms had been a great decision. Dominic slept on his side,
his head nestled into the curve of Evrain's neck. Only his
fluttering eyelids betrayed the fact that his dreams were not
peaceful. Evrain was exhausted yet found himself unable to
sleep even with the warmth of Dominic's bare skin pressed
against him. Gregory's plan rolled over and over in his
mind like the slow replay of a black and white movie. He
stroked Dominic's hair and found that the action calmed
his racing thoughts a little. Dominic's breathing seemed to
steady as he continued his gentle ministrations, winding
and unwinding tendrils of dark red silk. So much had
happened in the last twenty-four hours and a confusion of
images filled his head. It was impossible to relax. He felt

so protective of Dominic—he knew that his attitude and actions were often unreasonable but he was still unable to prevent his dominant side from emerging. Dominic was shy and quiet but he could also be stubborn. His gentle strength was the much needed counterpoint to Evrain's fiery nature. Theirs was a perfect partnership and Evrain was petrified that Dominic would run from a world that must be terrifying for him at times.

Evrain couldn't deny that he was scared himself. He was still very inexperienced, still learning to control the immense power that he could often feel boiling within himself. Back in the underground garage he had come very close to losing his grip on his belief, that he should never use his power to harm others. His anger at Symeon had threatened to overtake all sense of reason. Only the sound of Dominic's voice had brought him back from that dark place.

He drifted into a doze but remained aware. Time moved on and there was a subtle change in the light as the sun rose above the trees outside. A chorus of birds kept up their symphony in the garden. It was all so normal, the way he wanted it to be every day, but he knew it couldn't last. With the covers pulled down to his waist, Dominic's creamy skin was irresistible. Evrain breathed in the scent of greenery that always seemed to surround his lover. Beneath the quilt he found the firm curve of Dominic's ass. He stroked the top of his thigh then into the crease that led to his groin. His smooth skin radiated heat. Evrain nudged the covers lower. He couldn't resist circling his fingers around Dominic's hardening shaft.

He squeezed lightly, regretting that Dominic's position meant he couldn't reach back to cup the weight of his balls. Dominic mumbled something into his neck but didn't seem to be totally conscious. Evrain twitched his lips into a smile. Dominic was adorable. The warmth of Evrain's love for him welled through his body, making his heart pound faster. He could hardly believe how lucky he was to have earned Dominic's trust and love. It was a gift beyond price.

Sighing with contentment, Evrain turned his attention back to his boyfriend's stiff cock and began to squeeze and stroke alternately. Dominic moaned and rolled onto his back, parting his legs to allow Evrain better access. Evrain grinned and stroked harder, feathering his fingers around the root then squeezing the tip so that tiny beads of pre-cum spread like oil beneath his fingertips. Dominic's muscles tensed under his touch and knew that he must now be awake even though he was still feigning sleep. Evrain moved his hand more quickly until his injured wrist began to ache from the rapid pumping action. Dominic's lips parted. His copper lashes fluttered, revealing glints of blue.

"Don't stop," Dominic whispered.

"Not asleep then?" Evrain slowed his movements, teasing Dominic with feather light touches.

"Hardly. Evrain...please!"

Evrain responded to the desperate plea. He tugged on Dominic's rigid cock with sure movements. When he came, Dominic's ass lifted from the bed and his spine arched, thrusting his groin into the air. Glistening cream spattered Evrain's hand and Dominic's taut stomach until he finally relaxed with a gratified sigh.

Evrain kicked the bed covers off the end of the bed because they were tangling around his feet. He positioned himself so that he could lift Dominic's legs over his shoulders. He pulled Dominic's knees wide apart and bent him back, leaning over him. Dominic gazed up at him with calm acceptance, a smile playing over his lips. Belatedly, Evrain realized how sore Dominic had been earlier that day. He didn't want to hurt him, nor did he want to forego the pleasure of sinking into his welcoming heat.

He channeled, commanding the air to his will. He formed a cushioning sleeve around his cock. Drawing moisture from the air he made the sleeve slick, then pressed home his claim. Dominic's eyes widened but there was no sign he was in any pain. Evrain stilled, waiting for his lover's body to adjust to his size, but his patience wasn't matched by Dominic, who banged his fist on the mattress and shouted, "Move!"

Evrain bent him double as he sank inside him to his full length then withdrew almost to his tip before plunging back in again. Dominic seemed to gasp, whimper, scream and laugh at the same time, as Evrain repeated the process again and again until he could hold himself back no longer. As he came, the cushion of air and water dissipated. Evrain panted through his release, his gaze firmly fixed on Dominic's blue eyes.

Aftershocks rocked them both until eventually Evrain softened and slid from Dominic's body, lowering his lover's legs to the bed. They clung together in a close hug and Evrain ruffled his dark red hair with affection. "For some reason I couldn't wait to get my hands on you. This atmosphere of danger is making me horny."

"You did something. You felt bigger somehow."

"I didn't want to hurt you. I tried something new with a cushion of air. Did it feel good?"

"Sure did."

"I suppose we should get up." Evrain didn't want to move. "Gregory is bound to call soon. I don't want him to think that all we do when we're alone together is fuck."

Dominic groaned. "You know, just for a moment I had forgotten about everything going on. It was nice while it lasted." Dominic got out of bed. He padded over to the window. With a jerk, he twitched the curtain aside and looked down the garden toward the gate. He turned back toward the bed. "It seems that Imelda has called off her dogs for now. There's no one there."

"That probably means that Gregory has made some kind of arrangement with her," Evrain surmised. "We'd better get dressed in case he shows up at the door. Of course, if you don't put some clothes on fast you're unlikely to get out of this bedroom anytime soon." He leered. Watching Dominic without any clothes on was one of Evrain's favorite pastimes.

They took it in turns to shower and dress. Dominic went first then headed for the kitchen to put together a snack from whatever he could find in the cupboards. Evrain took his time, wandering naked from the bathroom to the bedroom only to find Shadow spread out on the bed. Evrain felt a strange need to cover up. He grabbed a T-shirt then held it over his groin. Shadow groomed herself, her eyes following him as if he were a plump mouse.

"Grandma, is that really you?" Evrain felt stupid talking to the cat but he was already half convinced Agatha's spirit inhabited the animal. Shadow rolled onto her back, legs in the air, tail twitching. "I'm going to take that as a yes." He rubbed Shadow's soft belly. "Gregory knew all along. I think maybe I didn't want to admit it, but I'm glad you're here. Back to look out for me, huh?"

"Meow."

"Or to keep an eye on me?" Purrs rumbled through the prone animal. "I'd appreciate you not lying in wait to catch me naked. Or Dominic. Got it?"

Shadow ignored him, apparently deciding it was time for a bath. She licked at one paw. Evrain grabbed his clothes then made his escape. Shadow had staked her claim on the bedroom and he wasn't going to argue. He dressed on the landing then padded barefoot down the stairs.

"I defrosted some vegetable soup." Dominic called. "When this…crisis… is over we are going to have to do the mother of all grocery runs. We're out of almost everything."

Evrain dissolved into laughter and found he couldn't stop. He wiped the tears from his eyes. "How did this happen? We're discussing grocery shopping before facing a coven of blood-lusting witches while our possessed cat has turned out to be a voyeur." He collapsed into a chair. "It's a dream sequence, isn't it? I'm going to wake up soon. Like one of those terrible soaps Grandma used to love."

"You're getting hysterical," Dominic said, placing a steaming bowl of soup in front of him. "There's no bread left, I'm afraid."

"That's okay. My stomach's churning anyway."

"And what's that about Shadow?"

"Never mind." Evrain spooned up some soup. "Probably best you don't know."

Dominic shrugged before taking a seat with his food. He'd just lifted his spoon when Evrain's phone rang. Evrain froze. "This is it, I suppose."

"So answer it." Dominic sounded a good deal calmer than Evrain felt. His skin itched. He snatched up the phone.

"Brookes."

"That's a strange way to answer the phone, Evrain."

"Oh, hi, Gregory. Sorry. Wasn't thinking. My brain probably decided I was in the office."

"Are we on loudspeaker?"

"Should we be?"

"Well, it will save you repeating everything for Dominic."

Evrain pressed the appropriate button. "Go ahead. We're listening."

"This won't take long. I don't think there's any need for us to come back out to the cottage. I've made an arrangement with Imelda."

Evrain swallowed. "Okay."

"You will provide the blood she requires. In return, she will leave you alone. Members of the Octis Coven will observe. She has agreed that Nathaniel and I can also be present."

"You trust her?"

"In this, I think I do. This way, she gets what she wants. The Coven witness her success, consolidating her position as leader. And she avoids any more destruction of Octis property. She won't be so careless this time," he said. "Yesterday's fiasco damaged the trust that the coven members had in her ability to act in their interest."

Gregory's words sent a chill through Evrain's body. The situation was becoming more and more dangerous. "I'm concerned how they will react when they discover that all the trouble they're going to is for nothing."

"I don't think we have any other option."

"Well, it's too late to change anything now. In a few hours it will all be over one way or another."

"Very well. There's a developed parking area on the south side of the highway at Beacon Rock. Do you know it?"

Evrain looked at Dominic, who nodded. "I don't but Dominic does. We'll find it."

"We'll see you there just before sunset. It's set back from the road and little used in the evening. It's neutral ground. Accessible to everyone and private enough for our purposes."

"Very well. I want Nathaniel there to protect Dominic."

"He'll be there."

"I want to spend some time scouting the area to make sure we have an escape route should we need it. So we'll get there a bit earlier to check the spot out. You realize this won't just be a case of using a sterile needle and a test tube, Evrain?"

"Not dramatic enough?" Evrain asked.

"A ceremonial knife will be used to open a vein and a small amount of blood will be allowed to drip into a copper goblet. You'll have to be channeling at the time. I suggest that the simplest thing to concentrate on would be the creation of a small flame. Coryn will stand with Dominic because I may have to channel too. Nathaniel will protect them both if it becomes necessary."

"As plans go," Evrain said, "this one isn't great but it's the best we have."

There wasn't anything else to say. Evrain ended the call. The remains of his soup had gone cold but he ate it anyway. He pushed his dish away then reached for Dominic's hand. He wasn't going to admit to being scared but Dominic was intuitive enough to know it. Dominic's touch and his understanding silence were comforting.

Chapter Fourteen

After arriving at the designated meeting point, Dominic found a spot to wait with Coryn and Damon. While Gregory, Nathaniel and Evrain discussed their plans and circled the site again and again, considering every eventuality, he, Coryn and an unusually subdued Damon sat on one of the huge boulders at the edge of the lot, watching them. Dominic turned to Coryn, smiling. "I'm sorry Evrain gave you both so much grief about the agrimony over dinner yesterday."

Coryn chuckled. "Well, he didn't lose his temper completely, though I think Gregory's ears were burning for a while. Did Evrain give you a hard time?"

Dominic swallowed as he remembered. "Yes, quite hard, you could say that."

Coryn stared at him curiously then grinned. "Ah, I see."

"He was more upset with himself than me. He just couldn't express it properly. He feels guilty for getting himself caught by Symeon. He thinks that led to all this."

"It did, in a way," Coryn said. "But sooner or later Imelda would have taken more drastic steps. At least this way we have a modicum of control." Coryn tilted his head back, gazing at the cloudless sky. "Are you scared about what's going to happen later?"

Dominic ran his fingers over the sparkling granite they were sitting on and chewed his lower lip. "I'm scared for Evrain. I just want this all to be over so that we can get back to some kind of a normal life. I'm just a gardener."

Coryn put a comforting hand on his shoulder and squeezed. "I think you need to face up to the truth that a life with Evrain is always going to be anything but normal."

Dominic thought about that statement as they sat together in quiet companionship watching their respective partners pace around, deep in conversation. The time went by far too fast and it wasn't long before the sun began to sink below the horizon. There were a few dense stands of trees dotted around but the parking area was situated on a flat plain in the river valley. There was an expansive view to the south. The sky turned vermillion and amber, then pink. Heavy gray shadows fell across the area. Small pieces of crystal in the rocks caught the light and glittered. On any other day, Dominic would have been able to appreciate the beauty of it, but today the dark shadows just seemed ominous and the red light spread a hint of hell across the landscape.

He drew in a sharp breath. In the distance he could see the lights of a cavalcade of vehicles approaching their way down the road. He counted five cars, all proceeding at a measured pace. They turned into the parking area then drew up in a semicircle on one side opposite where Gregory and Evrain had parked.

Coryn drew Dominic and Damon away and they stood, half concealed behind a small copse of trees. Nathaniel jogged across to wait with them. He put his arm around Damon's waist, drawing him close.

Gregory and Evrain waited in the center of the clearing, their silhouettes outlined in gold. Imelda was the first to leave her vehicle. If Dominic had been expecting flowing robes and pointy hats, he was disappointed. Imelda was wearing well-cut black trousers and a thick dark red sweater, which seemed to hint at her lust for blood. The eight women who came to join her were less dramatically dressed—one or two were young and attractive, but the rest were completely unremarkable. Under normal circumstances, no one would have given them a second glance and there was no way of knowing that together they formed the most powerful Coven in the northwest. Most of them cast covetous glances toward Evrain as they moved to stand in a loose circle.

Gregory took Evrain by the hand then led him to the center of the circle, where he gestured for him to kneel. Evrain dropped to the ground and looked up at his godfather, waiting for the signal to begin.

"Why is he kneeling?" Dominic whispered.

"Because he has to be stable when he channels and he may not be when Gregory cuts his palm. It's also part of the show for Imelda. Gregory wants Evrain to come across as less of a threat than he actually is. Perception is everything."

"Imelda, do you have the knife and goblet?" Gregory asked. The evening was clear and still. The sound of his voice carried to where Dominic, with a clear line of sight, waited with the others.

Imelda approached Gregory. She extended a simple dagger of gray steel. From what Dominic could see, its handle was not ornate — there were no jewels or mysterious designs that caught the light. The fact that it was clearly a tool, designed to be efficient and useful, made it all the more horrifying to Dominic as he looked on. The copper goblet she handed over was very similar, made from plain, unadorned metal.

Imelda took a few steps backward but not so far away that she couldn't see exactly what was going on. Evrain extended his arm, allowing Gregory to grip his wrist loosely. With his free hand Evrain began to make gestures and muttered the simple incantation that allowed him to manipulate fire.

Dominic shuddered as Evrain began to channel. He locked his knees, accepting the deep-seated ache that always came with Evrain's use of his power. Coryn put an arm around his shoulders but said nothing. Damon gave him an understanding nod.

Evrain was absolutely focused on what he was doing and a small, delicate flame hovered in the air above his outstretched hand. A perfect tapered shape, it was blue at the base, deep orange at the center, fading to silver at the tip where wisps of dark smoke disappeared into the air. Perhaps it was a side effect of the channeling but Dominic could see every detail and hear every word with absolute clarity. As Evrain continued to whisper words of power, Gregory took the knife and made a small incision in his palm, beneath the flame. Evrain didn't falter as Gregory turned his hand over and allowed deep red droplets of blood to fall into the goblet. To Dominic, time slowed as drop after drop splashed into the metal cup.

"This is taking forever," he muttered. Coryn patted his shoulder.

"It will. A drop of blood is not much. It will take a while to even half fill the goblet."

Finally Gregory curled Evrain's fingers into a fist and patted his arm. "You may stop now, Evrain."

The flame disappeared with a soft pop and Evrain relaxed with an audible sigh of relief. He remained on his knees and watched Gregory hand the goblet to Imelda. Dominic could almost feel the wet warmth of blood squeezing between his fingers and the throbbing pain of the cut on his hand.

"I hope you're satisfied that we have done everything as you requested, Imelda. Now conduct your tests and we can finish this once and for all." Gregory sounded cold and stern.

Dominic wanted to run to Evrain but he held his position. Nathaniel took a step away from Damon, his entire body poised and alert.

"You expecting trouble?" Coryn whispered.

"Something feels wrong." Nathaniel swiveled around, checking every direction, but the light was fading and it was hard to see. "There's a vague scent on the winds...I can't quite pin it down. Smells like rot."

"Imelda's taking the goblet." Dominic held his breath. He had to let it out eventually but breathing seemed an irrelevance under the circumstances.

Imelda's eyes had narrowed at Gregory's icy tone, but she took the cup and handed it to another woman, who walked away toward one of the vehicles. She was perhaps halfway between Imelda and the car when a dark figure appeared from nowhere, grabbed the goblet from her grasp then threw her to the ground where she lay unmoving. Imelda's cry of outrage was silenced as the mysterious figure walked toward her.

"That's Symeon!" Damon cried.

"Fuck. He used a concealment spell. That must have been his stench I detected." Nathaniel edged forward, herding everyone else behind him. Dominic eased sideways. He wanted to keep a line of sight on Evrain.

"Symeon." Gregory's flat tone showed no surprise.

"How the hell did you get here, Malus?" Imelda wasn't as restrained. She spoke with barely suppressed fury.

"It seems you do not have as firm a grip on power within the Octis Coven as you thought, my dear."

The oil slick of Symeon's voice made Dominic want to wretch.

"Some of your revered colleagues are contemplating a change of leadership. They have been giving me what you would not, including the handy spell that got me here unnoticed."

Evrain made to stand.

"No. You stay put. I like you on your knees."

Dominic was glad he couldn't make out Evrain's expression.

Symeon dipped a finger into the goblet then withdrew it, coated in glistening red. He put it to his lips, tasting the blood with relish. He frowned, taking another lick, before his features tightened with anger.

"Agrimony! You poisoned him with agrimony." He cast the goblet aside, spilling the precious contents onto the ground. Imelda screamed and jumped forward, grasping desperately at the cup as it rolled away from her.

"It's useless, you stupid bitch," Symeon snapped. "I don't know how they did it but his blood is tainted. This is your fault. If you'd left it to me this would never have happened."

Imelda got to her feet. "If I'd left it to you, Symeon, Evrain and Dominic would both be dead and we would have nothing. As it is, it seems that we have *both* been outwitted." She gave Gregory a wry nod. "I don't suppose you'd care to tell me how you did it?"

"No." Gregory didn't smile. "But be assured that Evrain's blood will never be of any use to you."

Imelda turned to the women now gathered behind her. "Sisters, resolving our differences is not something that should be done in the company of warlocks. Octis should conduct its business in private. I apologize for wasting your time, but we will reconvene at the usual place at dawn."

Symeon didn't seem bothered as the women melted one by one into the darkness, taking their fallen colleague with them. He waited as car engines started up and the vehicles moved away. Imelda remained where she was.

Gregory glared at Symeon. "You never give up, do you? Even you can't be so stupid as to think you stand a chance against three of us. You are no longer of use to the Coven, power struggle or not. Without their potions you are impotent."

Dominic was sure the choice of descriptor was deliberate.

"Well, that just depends now, doesn't it?" Symeon grabbed Imelda and pulled her against his chest. From beneath his long, black coat he pulled a gun. "For once I agree with you. I'm not stupid. But this gives me an advantage, don't you think?" He pressed the barrel of the gun to the side of Imelda's neck.

"What makes you think I give a damn about what happens to her?" Gregory asked.

"Oh, I'm sure you don't really care. However, your ridiculous sense of morality will not allow you to see a woman harmed, however much of a bitch she is, if you can prevent it."

"And can I prevent it?"

"Of course. I'm not fond of littering the landscape with corpses."

Nathaniel shunted Dominic backward. He tugged Damon along too.

"Symeon must know we're here, Nathaniel, but not Damon," Dominic whispered.

Nathaniel gave him a sharp look. "What are you saying?"

"Damon should hide. He may be able to help."

"I don't want him putting himself in danger. He's not wearing that stab vest this evening."

"You have to let me do it, Sir." Damon was already moving deeper into the trees. "We need any advantage we can get."

Dominic understood why Nathaniel was so torn, but eventually the warlock nodded and Damon slipped away. Dominic turned his attention back to the clearing.

"Bring the rest of your friends over here, Gregory. They must be feeling left out."

Even though he could hear Symeon's command, Nathaniel waited until he got a signal from Gregory before moving. Dominic and Coryn walked behind him until they were next to Gregory and Evrain.

"Well, isn't this nice? All four warlocks together in one place. Much as I'm enjoying the company, you, Gregory, are going to leave. You'll take Nathaniel and Coryn with you. Dominic, get on your knees beside Evrain."

"No!" Evrain shouted.

Symeon fired the gun into the ground in front of Evrain. "How many deaths do you want on your conscience, Evrain?"

Dominic dropped to his knees. He grabbed Evrain's hand.

"Oh, how sweet." Symeon moved the gun back to Imelda's temple. "Now, I want you, Coryn and Nathaniel to make your way over to your car, get in it then drive away. I can see the lights from here. Once you are a suitable distance away I will let this silly bitch go." He pulled back the hammer on the gun with an audible click. "Do as I say or I pull the trigger and believe me, I won't hesitate."

Evrain cast a panicked look at Gregory. "I won't sacrifice

Dominic for this woman after what she's done to us. No moral code is worth this. Let him shoot her. He won't have time to get to the rest of us and I'll fry him where he stands."

"No you won't, you little upstart. I'm not quite as powerless as you all seem to think." Symeon twitched the fingers of his free hand. Blue flames writhed around his fingers.

"That potion will wear off soon enough, Symeon."

Dominic twitched as Evrain channeled, matching Symeon flame for flame. Gregory put a restraining hand on his shoulder. "Evrain, you're better than that. It may seem like what you want to do right now in the heat of the moment, but how would you live with it? This isn't the person you are and it's not the person that Dominic would want you to be."

"That's right." Dominic added his agreement.

Gregory squeezed Evrain's shoulder. "Have faith, boy. Take the right path now or you will regret it for the rest of your life."

"Very touching. Now leave before I get overexcited and shoot something just for the hell of it." The red in Symeon's eyes darkened.

Dominic took in the expressions of his friends. Gregory was somber, Coryn calm. Nathaniel looked like he wanted to create a tornado to swallow Symeon *and* Imelda. The three men walked slowly away. Dominic listened to the car's engine start up then the crunch of tires in gravel as it pulled away down the lane. Even though he knew it wasn't the case, he had a sense of abandonment. It seemed that he and Evrain were on their own. He hoped Damon stayed hidden and didn't try anything stupid. He didn't have any power. He was just flesh and blood. He could be hurt.

Symeon gave Imelda a sharp shove, making her stagger then drop to one knee. "Get out of here. Threaten me again and I will come after every single one of the bitches in your fucking coven. Believe me, I won't stop until you are all gone and your little girl's club will be a distant memory. I have more allies than you know."

Imelda had the sense to keep her mouth shut. She stood, brushed the dust from her pants then staggered away toward her car. Once she was gone, only one vehicle remained — the car Evrain and Dominic had arrived in. Dominic guessed Symeon must have some form of transport hidden close by. It wasn't as if he'd flown in on a broomstick.

When Symeon moved the gun to point at his head, Dominic flinched. Once more he was proving to be Evrain's weakness. If it weren't for him, Evrain could call the elements and bury Symeon like the worm he was. Dominic bit his lip. He squeezed Evrain's hand, trying to convey his love, his regret and his shame for being such a liability.

"It seems that yet again I have the upper hand, Evrain. This time you won't get away from me." Symeon laughed. "By poisoning your blood, you've reduced your value and now all I have left is revenge — and it will be sweet."

"You're insane, Symeon. Why don't you retire gracefully and use the little power you have left for good?"

"Preaching doesn't suit you, Evrain. Leave it to Gregory — his moralizing is enough for all of us. You're not like him. You're different. Much more like me in fact."

In Dominic's hand, Evrain's fingers felt ice-cold.

"I'm nothing like you," Evrain spat.

Symeon shrugged. "We'll see. Our experiences color the way we live our lives. Before I kill you, I'm going to make you watch while I violate your lover. I'm going to do things to him that you couldn't even begin to imagine. And when you're gone, I'll keep doing it until he can't even remember his own name, let alone yours."

Dominic felt the slight vibration that always preceded Evrain's channeling. Evrain was poised and ready to move the moment Symeon dropped his guard but the white haired warlock seemed full of purpose.

The gun didn't waver for an instant.

Symeon moved behind Dominic. He pulled him to his feet by his hair. Evrain started to rise but Symeon gave him a vicious kick to the ribs, causing him to collapse back to the ground. Pulling Dominic a few feet away, Symeon then slid one arm around his waist to undo the button on his pants then slide down the zipper. He thrust his hand down the front of his pants, all the while pressing the gun into his neck. A single tear rolled down Dominic's face as Symeon gripped his shaft, digging his nails into the tender flesh.

"Like some pain, don't you?" Symeon hissed.

Evrain's lips were compressed to a thin line, his green-gold eyes glowing as he was forced to watch the violation. Dominic thought it might be worth getting shot just to get Symeon's hand off him. He felt frozen by indecision. If he struggled Symeon might turn the gun on Evrain. If he didn't, Evrain might hate him.

Behind him, a twig snapped. Evrain had given no indication that anyone was approaching and Dominic marveled at his composure. Symeon kept a tight hold on him and the gun didn't move as he turned to face the newcomer. Damon walked toward them, hands held out to show that they were empty.

"Damon." Symeon's voice reflected curiosity. "How the hell did you get here?" He removed his hand from Dominic's pants. "Seen the light and decided to come back to me?"

Damon smiled. "I've been here a while. Watching. Listening." He blinked.

"And you've recovered from your injuries? I searched for you in the parking garage, but you'd gone."

"I didn't think you cared."

Symeon's focus was entirely on Damon. Dominic didn't dare move. He realized that Symeon had no idea Damon had helped him and Evrain escape the Octis building and that could give them the advantage they needed.

"Where the hell did you materialize from?" Symeon snarled. "Never mind. I'm glad you've made an appearance. I'm sure you will enjoy the show as much as I will. I may even give you a turn with this one." He yanked Dominic's hair.

Evrain began to channel. Dominic tried to draw attention away from him by struggling as much as possible. He kicked at Symeon's shins with his heels, making contact at least once. He tried to elbow him in the ribs, then bite at his arm. Symeon cuffed him hard.

"Keep still. My trigger finger is itchy and I'd prefer you to be in one piece when I fuck you."

The dust swirled around Dominic's feet, moving almost like eddies in a stream. Using all his strength he pulled away from Symeon, throwing himself to the ground. Lightning cracked, striking the dirt just in front of Symeon's highly polished boots. He was thrown into the air, landing heavily several feet away. The gun skimmed across the ground, bouncing several times. Dominic rolled onto his belly but stayed down. He didn't want to get in Evrain's way while he was still channeling. There was a rumble of thunder then a deluge began. The rain hammered down, pounding dust into mud in an instant. Dominic was soon soaked. In the darkness and through the torrential rain, he could barely see what was happening. Symeon was trying to get to his feet, but could get no purchase in the mud. Damon scrambled for the gun. Evrain held his arms aloft, focused on commanding all four elements.

The sound of a gunshot penetrated the natural cacophony, the loud retort shocking. Dominic could make out Damon kneeling on the ground next to Symeon's prone form. Dominic crawled over to him, barely feeling the stones cutting into his knees and hands. The perfectly round hole in Symeon's forehead and his sightless red eyes betrayed what Damon had done.

Damon hugged himself, rocking back and forth. The discarded gun was half buried in the mud at his side. Dominic threw his arms around Damon and held him tight, absorbing the tremors from his light body. Damon sobbed against his shoulder, his tears mingling with the rain.

When Evrain stopped channeling, Dominic's body sagged

with relief. The rain had petered out but it would be a while before the drips from his sodden hair ceased rolling down his face. Evrain came into view behind Damon.

"Damon grabbed the gun and shot him. Symeon's dead," Dominic said more calmly than he felt.

"I can't say I'm sorry." Evrain's voice was cold as ice. "He did what I couldn't. Is he okay?"

"Just shocked, I think. He's soaked and cold. We should get him to the car."

"Gregory's car just pulled in. They must have turned around as soon as they were out of sight. Nathaniel will want to take care of Damon."

Damon scrubbed a muddy hand across his face, leaving dirty smears behind.

"Why did you do it, Damon?" Dominic asked.

"He would have killed Evrain and he was planning to do awful things to you, Dominic. You're my friends. You've done more for me than anyone ever has. I couldn't let that happen. Symeon was evil. He hurt everyone he came into contact with."

"Most of all you…" Dominic's heart broke for Damon.

There was the crunch of tires over gravel then the sound of running. Nathaniel skidded to a halt next to Dominic. He glanced at Symeon's corpse then at the gun.

"I'll take him, Dominic." Nathaniel bent then lifted Damon to his feet. "I'm here. Everything's going to be okay." He pulled Damon into a tight embrace.

Dominic scrambled to his feet just as Coryn and Gregory arrived.

"What happened?" Gregory asked.

"Damon shot Symeon," Dominic explained, reaching for Evrain's hand.

"Damon distracted Symeon enough that I could channel," Evrain explained. "I would have killed him I think… I was desperate enough and even with the potion Symeon was too weak to stand a chance against me. Damon saved me from having to."

"Good riddance," Coryn said with feeling.

"I'm afraid I have to agree." Gregory nodded. "Symeon Malus has been a thorn in my backside for far too long. He was always a poor excuse for a warlock. Power-crazy, money-grubbing, psychotic…"

"We get the picture, love." Coryn stopped the tirade.

"So do we call the cops?" Dominic asked.

"This is warlock business," Gregory replied. "Evrain, can you saturate the ground with enough water that it liquefies? I can help."

"I'll turn it to soup if I have to," Evrain said.

Dominic moved to stand with Coryn as the two warlocks channeled. He watched the already sodden ground around Symeon's body shimmer and shift. A couple of air bubbles rose to the surface then popped. Symeon and the gun sank from view, the mud closing over him.

"Now separate water and earth," Gregory ordered, fingers flickering.

Evrain frowned, muttering words Dominic couldn't quite hear. Where Symeon's body had lain, the ground dried and solidified. In less than a minute there was no evidence that a body had lain there at all.

"We pushed him deep." Gregory flexed his fingers. "There's no chance some wild critter will dig him up."

It was Coryn who diffused the tense atmosphere. "Well, I for one am starving and ready for my bed. I suggest we all head to wherever home is for the night."

"Good idea," Dominic agreed. He was about ready to collapse. The lure of a warm bed and Evrain's bare skin against his was irresistible. He tugged Evrain's hand.

"Is it really over?" Evrain said, sounding shattered.

"Yes, it is, love." Dominic couldn't imagine how Evrain was feeling. "Let's go home. Tomorrow is soon enough to think about all this." When he moved toward the car, Evrain followed. Dominic gave a brief wave to Gregory and Coryn. For now, all he wanted to do was be there for whatever Evrain needed.

Epilogue

For the next few days, Hornbeam Cottage was an oasis of tranquility. An anonymous call to Portland PD had drawn their attention to an abandoned car near a local beauty spot. Imelda and the Octis Coven had gone to ground, melting back into their lives as if nothing had ever happened. From what Gregory had discovered Imelda had held on to her position by the tips of her lacquered fingernails. It would be a while before she caused mischief again.

After staying one final night in Portland, Gregory and Coryn had departed for Florida amid promises to return soon. Gregory's parting words to Evrain had been, "Keep practicing. I've clearly underestimated your abilities. You'll have to work much harder the next time we meet." Evrain had repeated them to Dominic in the expectation of sympathy, but had gotten none.

Nathaniel and Damon had taken the company jet home. Talking to Dominic on the phone, Damon had confessed that he fully intended to join the mile high club—even though Felix would be traveling with them. Evrain knew the bravado was a cover. Damon would need all Nathaniel's care and attention for quite some time, to get over what had happened.

Evrain sat at the kitchen table, Shadow purring in his lap, while Dominic brewed some tea. Evrain had found the protective pendant where it had dropped, outside the garden gate, and it was now safely back around Dominic's neck, though Evrain wanted to replace the cord with a nice, heavy padlocked chain.

"You think Damon will be okay?" Dominic asked,

handing over a mug of steaming liquid that smelt mildly of apricots.

"He'll be fine. Nathaniel will make sure of that. Who'd have thought Damon would turn out to be our most valuable ally?"

"And a good friend."

Evrain nodded, then frowned. "What's this?" He held up his mug.

"Agrimony tea. Gregory said you need to keep drinking it for a while to make sure your blood stays tainted." Dominic stood over him expectantly, waiting for him to drink.

Evrain took a small sip. He grimaced. "Ugh! It's disgusting!"

"Drink it. All of it." Dominic sounded threatening. "We may have seen the last of the Coven, and Symeon is no more, but there's probably a queue of goblins, demons and orcs at the gate, just waiting to get their claws into you."

Evrain almost choked on his tea. He laughed. "Orcs?"

Dominic scowled. "Who the hell knows where you're concerned?"

Evrain sipped the tea and tried to get the image of the denizens of Middle Earth rampaging around the vegetable patch out of his head. He didn't quite manage to keep the humor from his eyes and when he looked up a strange expression crossed Dominic's face. He turned on his heel then walked out into the garden, closing the door behind him.

For a moment Evrain just sat with his hands wrapped around his mug. He fought back a sense of panic. Of fear. It was obvious now that Dominic had been deeply affected by their run-in with the Coven and with Symeon. It was too easy to ignore that every day Dominic had to believe the unbelievable, to accept a world that only a few months earlier had been the stuff of fantasy novels. If that wasn't enough, he was also expected to submit to a partner who could atomize him with a few flicks of his fingers.

Evrain put his head on his arms and groaned. "You

dumbass, selfish bastard." He had no doubt that Dominic loved him, he knew deep in his soul that it was true and it was proven every time he channeled. But he had never asked whether any of that love was rooted in fear. He had no misconceptions about his nature—he was demanding, possessive and seriously overprotective. Every time he looked at Dominic he had an overwhelming urge to keep him safe and well away from anyone who might dare to desire him.

His pushed his chair back abruptly then stood. It was time to show Dominic just how much he was loved.

Evrain found Dominic sitting on the stump of an ancient oak at the far end of the garden, head in his hands. He looked so miserable and Evrain's heart broke at the sight of him. He made no attempt to conceal his approach, but Dominic didn't look up until Evrain laid a hand on his shoulder. Beneath his touch, Evrain could feel Dominic shaking. "Are you crying?" He didn't wait for Dominic to answer, but dropped to his knees on the damp ground in front of him. He took Dominic's cold hands in his.

"I'm so sorry, Dominic. I should have taken a moment to consider how all this has been making you feel. Please come inside and give me a chance to show you how much I love you." Bright blue eyes, shiny with unshed tears, looked up at him.

"You don't have to do that, Evrain, I'll be fine in a little while. I suppose I'm just finding it hard to believe that we're finally safe and that there isn't some new monster lurking out of sight just around the corner. It's stupid, I know it is, but I feel that I'm missing something, a hint of something in the corner of my eye that I can't quite see."

Evrain squeezed his hands. "It's not stupid at all, it just shows how much you care, and I can't promise that there won't ever be another Symeon, another Coven. It's a dangerous world that I've dragged you into, but I can't let you go, Dominic, I can't face it without you."

A tear rolled down Dominic's smooth cheek. "You don't

have to. Don't you understand how much I love you?"

Evrain kissed away the tears, then brushed Dominic's soft lips with his own. "Come inside, you idiot, don't make me ask you again." He had judged the moment well. Dominic responded to the command in his tone and the gentle tug on his hands. Obediently, he followed him into the house and up to their bedroom.

"Sit down, don't say anything yet." Evrain took a deep breath and unbuttoned his shirt. He put it onto the back of a chair then slipped out of his pants, folding them carefully. He was wearing a pair of clinging black shorts that could not hide his arousal. He concealed his trembling hands by using them to roll down his shorts, then stepped out of them. For a moment he stood looking at Dominic, who was chewing on his lower lip, his eyes firmly fixed on Evrain's jutting cock.

Heart pounding, Evrain turned and bent over the side of the bed, a position that he had put Dominic in so many times before. He didn't speak — he didn't need to. He waited patiently and listened to the sounds of Dominic removing his clothes. The first touch was a kiss, soft lips pressed against the curve of his ass, and it sent a jolt the entire length of his body. Dominic knelt behind him and nibbled his way from the top of his thigh to the base of Evrain's spine. He began to explore the valley between Evrain's cheeks with his tongue. Dominic used his hands to part them wider and grant him better access. Very, very gently he licked his way around the edge of Evrain's fluttering entrance. Every muscle in Evrain's legs turned to jelly. He couldn't stay silent any longer. He moaned as Dominic blew onto his damp skin. The cool sensation sent miniature bolts of lightning to his cock and his knees almost gave way.

The torture increased as Dominic pushed the point of his tongue into him. "Fuck me, Dominic, please, do it now!"

Dominic stood and reached for the pot of cool gel that stood on the bedside table. He scooped a blob onto his fingers then coated his cock until it glistened. Evrain watched with anticipation. Dominic dipped his fingers into the jar again. He smoothed more of the gel around Evrain's virgin pucker. Evrain jerked at the contact and sank his teeth into the bedcovers. He felt Dominic's strong, work-calloused hands grip his hips and the head of Dominic's cock made the lightest of contact with his ass.

"Are you sure about this, Evrain?" Dominic's voice was tight with nerves.

Evrain knew that any hint of hesitation on his part and Dominic would pull away. That was the last thing he wanted. He gave his answer with a backward thrust his hips and a grunt of pain as Dominic's cock entered his channel.

"Holy fuck!" His exclamation was muffled by the bedclothes that he was now fisting as both hands clenched and unclenched. "That burns!" He attempted to relax his resistant anal muscles. Dominic slipped deeper inside him, applying pressure to something that sent a thrill of pleasure through his body, allowing him to ignore, if not forget, the pain.

"Are you okay?" Dominic started to withdraw, but Evrain pushed back against him once more.

"Move! Or I swear I'll turn you into a fucking frog!"

Dominic renewed his grip. He began to move backward and forward at an agonizingly slow pace.

"Do you want to spend the rest of your natural life croaking on a lily pond? Move. Fucking. Faster." Evrain was grinding his ass backward but Dominic stilled.

"Still dominant, even in this situation. You can't do those kind of spells, so quit threatening me or I may have to spank you while I fuck you."

Dominic did as he was told anyway. He began to give Evrain's ass the pounding Evrain was desperate for. They almost knocked heads as Evrain's back arched and he gave a cry of ecstasy when Dominic found the sensitive bundle of nerves inside him with unerring accuracy.

"So good. Don't stop," Evrain ordered.

"You just can't help yourself, can you? What if I feel the

urge to torture you the way you do me?"

"You're too sweet and you love me," Evrain spluttered. He could hardly cope with the sensations building inside him.

"You love me too but you still edge me for hours," Dominic muttered and for a moment Evrain feared he'd created a sexual sadist. There was only room for one of those in their relationship and he had dibs on the position.

"Dominic…" he growled a warning.

Dominic reached beneath Evrain's straining thighs and grasped his cock. It was so hot. Evrain felt like he was on fire inside, and after only a couple of strokes his orgasm barreled through him and he came with a shout that was half ecstasy, half relief. Dominic slowed his movements a little. Evrain summoned the presence of mind to squeeze his inner muscles, gripping Dominic's cock. He could feel Dominic shaking as his orgasm overtook him. Then there was a warm gush of liquid in his channel and Dominic's body pressed over his back. Dominic took deep, heaving breaths, mumbling curses as his body trembled through a series of aftershocks.

Once Dominic slipped free of him, Evrain crawled onto the bed. He collapsed onto his belly, breathing heavily. He listened as Dominic padded across the landing to the bathroom before returning with a damp towel. It was alien to lie still while Dominic cleaned him up, but Evrain enjoyed it. It was nice to be the one taken care of for a change, and Dominic needed it.

When Dominic was finished, Evrain rolled onto his back. Dominic stretched out next to him and for a while they just lay together. Evrain's breathing slowed to normal. He got to his knees then climbed over Dominic. Straddling his thighs, he gazed down at him.

"You're so beautiful."

Dominic blushed.

"Now you can say that I am yours as much as you are mine. Do you trust me?"

"Yes." That single word was stated with absolute certainty.

Evrain leaned forward to kiss Dominic and as their lips touched he channeled.

"Your eyes are glowing," Dominic murmured. He stretched his arms above his head.

"Are they?"

"Uh-huh." Dominic twitched. "My skin's tingling."

"Does it hurt?"

"No, it's not painful. More a slight prickling feeling that itches a little."

Evrain held him in place. His own skin also burned but the sensation wasn't unpleasant.

"What have you done? I'm not a frog, am I?"

Evrain moved to lie next to him on the bed, propped up on one elbow.

"You already know I can't do that—though it would be a useful skill." He grinned. "Take a look at your arms."

Dominic sat up. He stared. Circling both wrists and climbing part way up the soft inner surface of his arms, silvery green tendrils of ivy decorated his skin. They looked very similar to the designs that Gregory had created with the agrimony. Not as defined as tattoos, the leaves and stems seemed to sit just below the surface of his skin.

"If you don't like them, I can take them away again," Evrain said anxiously. He touched his biceps, where a similar design curled around the flexing muscle in a band that circled his arm. Tiny ivy leaves also formed a ring around his third finger. Dominic looked down at a matching circle around his finger, and smiled.

A long, lingering kiss signaled Dominic's acceptance. Evrain stroked his chest and belly. "They look amazing on you. Now you'll always be under my spell."

Dominic's eyes lit from within. "Normal is overrated anyway."

Evrain laughed. Joy flooded through him. "I can't wait for our next adventure."

Dominic smacked him. "Don't tempt fate!"

"Why not? Maybe I enjoy living dangerously." A pillow smacked him in the head. From outside the bedroom door came an indignant yowl. "Okay, okay! I'm outnumbered. No more drama. At least for a little while." The last few words were barely more than a whisper.

Elemental Love

Excerpt

Chapter One

Twenty-one years ago…

"Closed doors, I hate closed doors. Why don't I have the power to see through them? That, at least, would be a useful ability." Three-hundred-year-old floorboards creaked as Gregory Thanet paced the galleried landing of Wenlock House. He walked up and down past three doors, each fashioned from heavy oak and furnished with black iron hinges and handles. Two stood ajar, revealing hints of unoccupied bedrooms, but the third was firmly closed, a solid barrier to unwanted intrusion and the cause of Gregory's current frustration.

"For goodness' sake, Gregory, you're wearing out the carpet. Be still." Gregory's companion leaned against the gallery rail and gave him an exasperated look.

Gregory paused his march briefly, shot a glare at the woman but then resumed his pacing with a grunt. "Leave me be, woman, I'll be still when we know that everything is as it should be."

"Nature moves at her own pace, you know that. There's no changing it—nor should we. What will be will be."

"Stop trying to sound like some wise and ancient soothsayer, Agatha. You're not helping and it doesn't suit you. The kid is a week late already—you'd think he would be keen to greet the world by now. When he's grown I'll remember that he kept me up half the night. I'm sure I'll get plenty of opportunities for revenge when he's older." Gregory stopped and folded his arms across his chest.

"I might not be able to see the future, Gregory Thanet, but even a complete idiot could have predicted that my grandson would arrive today."

Gregory examined his companion. Agatha looked tired. Her skin was quite smooth, marred only by a few laughter lines around her hazel eyes, eyes that still sparkled with warmth and intelligence. Her silver hair was swept smoothly back and fastened with a comb, intricately fashioned from beaten copper. She remained an attractive woman, who must have possessed great beauty in her youth, but she looked paler than usual and she rested her weight against the banister rather than standing in her usual ramrod-straight stance.

Gregory experienced a rare pang of guilt that he might be adding to his friend's worries. "All Hallows' Eve. There's a lot of power in the air right now."

Agatha cocked her head to one side and closed her eyes as if listening to sounds that only she could hear. "My grandson will be with us soon and there is little that you or I can do to change the course of his destiny." For a moment, a worried frown creased her forehead. "It is not certain that he will inherit the gift."

Gregory sighed. "In this, you deceive yourself, Agatha.

The calling has skipped a generation. History dictates that the next born will be unusually powerful and that power will be magnified even further in a male child."

"There has been no warlock in my family line for over five hundred years, only witches. Why are you so convinced that it will change now? We know of only three others living, Gregory. You, Symeon Malus and Constantine De Vries. It would be a chance in a billion."

Gregory scratched the tip of his long nose. "I should have bought a lottery ticket then. All the portents point to it, the date alone… It is time. Time the triangle became a square."

"I'm not sure Symeon Malus will ever be part of that square," Agatha said. "I don't see him as the cornerstone of anything with value or integrity."

"True, and if the child is born with the power, you and I will need to ensure that Symeon's gaze remains elsewhere." Gregory shivered. "I swear to the goddess, this country is the dampest place on earth. It's all right for you, Agatha, you live in the second dampest place on the planet. You're used to groping through fog. I want to get back to Florida. I need to — before I develop trench foot."

"Pah. What you really want is to get back to Coryn. You're a ship without an anchor when the two of you are apart. He could have come to see the child too, you know." Agatha grabbed a stray hair and pushed it back into a restraining grip.

"Coryn hates airplanes, you know that. I would never ask him to fly across the pond unless it was a life or death situation."

"If it were, you wouldn't have to ask him."

"He reckons that if men were designed to fly through the air, then human cannonball would be a much more popular career choice."

Agatha snorted. "I think his phobia is a myth. He just uses it as an excuse to get a few days' break from your—" She whistled and twiddled her fingers in the air.

Gregory rolled his eyes. "Twiddling your fingers that

way will get you turned into an aardvark. It takes practice to bend your digits into shapes imbued with power. After thirty-two years together, Coryn is more than capable of dealing with my—" He whistled. "As you so delicately put it."

Agatha snorted. "Men with magic! Whoever the hell thought that would be a good idea was seriously damaged." She shook her head slowly.

Gregory grinned and waggled a silver eyebrow.

The mewling cry of a newborn sounded from behind the closed bedroom door, and Agatha allowed her lips to curve into a smile.

"Well, it seems the waiting is over. I have a grandchild — and, from the sound of that bellowing, he's a fine, healthy boy."

"About damned time." Gregory grouched. He still smiled right along with Agatha.

Agatha crossed the landing and knocked softly on the door, which soon swung open to admit her. Gregory followed her inside, pushing down his excitement.

The bedroom was bathed in the cool light of a new dawn. The soft green of the walls seemed to shimmer and the wooden floor was burnished with gold. Gregory looked around in wonder, then dragged his gaze back to the bed.

"Lyssa, James—congratulations, my dears!" Agatha clapped her hands together in delight as she walked over to the bed.

Gregory hung back a little, giving her the privilege of first viewing.

Agatha's daughter, Lyssa, sat up in bed propped against a mound of pillows. She was pale, her eyes shadowed in the purple of exhaustion, but still she glowed with radiant happiness. A small bundle wrapped in a pale blue blanket rested in her arms. Her husband, James, sat nervously on the edge of the mattress, looking utterly shell-shocked but delighted as the midwife fussed around them.

Lyssa held the baby out to her mother with a smile. "His

name is Evrain. Evrain James Brookes. Hold him, Mum, isn't he beautiful?"

Gregory held his breath as Agatha reached for the small bundle and cradled the child in her arms. She pushed the blanket back from the baby's head, and a mop of thick black hair was revealed, sticking out in all directions.

"He is absolutely gorgeous, darling. Didn't you both do well!" Agatha stroked the child's hair.

Gregory moved in closer. Tiny fists punched at the air, so Gregory offered the boy his own hand. Immediately, the baby grabbed hold, wrapping his fingers around Gregory's offering with surprising strength. Gregory grinned at Agatha in delight, then looked back to the baby. His eyes were the dark blue of every newborn but, as Gregory focused his senses on the child, he could see that they would become dark green. Just a shade deeper than his own.

Cooing softly, Agatha muttered a lilting incantation and rocked the baby gently. To Lyssa and James, the song probably sounded like a lullaby, but Gregory knew a spell when he heard one. Tiny eyelids closed and the baby slept. Gregory's finger was released. After a few more minutes of cuddling, Agatha reluctantly returned the baby to his parents.

More books from
L.M. Somerton

Even the best-planned experiment can have unpredictable consequences.

Lucien Thorne likes to be in control, but the boy he wants to own may take some convincing.

WHAT'S *his* PASSION?

Brock and Kyle journey
together into a life
of adventure.

TESTING
LYSANDER

L M SOMERTON

Part of the What's his Passion? collection

Feel the fear and do it anyway.

Book three in the Investigating Love series

Can truth be found in the cards?

About the Author

L.M. Somerton

Lucinda lives in a small village in the English countryside, surrounded by rolling hills, cows and sheep. She started writing to fill time between jobs and is now firmly and unashamedly addicted.

She loves the English weather, especially the rain, and adores a thunderstorm. She loves good food, warm company and a crackling fire. She's fascinated by the psychology of relationships, especially between men, and her stories contain some subtle (and some not so subtle) leanings towards BDSM.

L.M. Somerton loves to hear from readers. You can find contact information, website details and an author profile page at https://www.pride-publishing.com/

www.ingramcontent.com/pod-product-compliance
Lightning Source LLC
Chambersburg PA
CBHW020424180626
46812CB00003B/1141